White Ghost

'I'm singing that song', Fitz boomed as he wiped a bead of perspiration off his forehead, 'and I've got the hairs coming up on the back of my neck.' He paused for a few, theatrical seconds. 'Why?'

None of the students knew why. Embarrassment, maybe?

'Because', said Fitz before anyone ventured an answer, 'the only time my father whistled that tune was when he tried to control his temper.' He paused again and looked at the sea of blank faces. Then he smiled. 'My father never *did* control his temper, so 'Distant Drums' was always the prelude to a slap around the head. *That*', he added with something akin to venom, 'is negative conditioning. I'd claim now that it made me a better person. It certainly made me a faster runner,' he said with a merry glint in his eye. 'But', continued Fitz as he held up a finger, 'it *could* have been the perfect *trigger* for a pathological mind. Some killers rely on the smallest of excuses to commit the most heinous crimes. And whistling 'Distant Drums' is not small; it could have acted as a highly effective trigger. By rights,' he said with another smile, 'I should be barking mad and angry.'

Tom McGregor is a journalist and author of fourteen books. He lives and works in London.

Tom McGregor

WHITE GHOST

Mandarin

A Mandarin Paperback

First published in Great Britain 1996
by Mandarin Paperbacks
an imprint of Reed International Books Ltd
Michelin House, 81 Fulham Road, London SW3 6RB
and Auckland, Melbourne, Singapore and Toronto

Cracker © Granada Television and Jimmy McGovern

Text Copyright © Tom McGregor 1996.
Adapted from a screenplay by Paul Abbott.
The author has asserted his moral rights.

A CIP catalogue record for this title
is available from the British Library
ISBN 0 7493 2339 6

Printed and bound in Great Britain
by Cox & Wyman Ltd, Reading, Berkshire

Prologue

Dr Edward Fitzgerald was hot. He attributed that, not without foundation, to the fact that he was in a sweltering, humid – he would go so far as to say horrible – climate. Others had been tempted to point out that as he was unfit, twenty-one stone, and a heavy smoker and drinker to boot, he was not best equipped to deal with high temperatures. Part of the reason why they stopped short of pointing that out was because Dr Fitzgerald, or Fitz as he insisted on being called, was also six foot two. His was an imposing presence. Especially in Hong Kong.

After nearly a week in the territory, Fitz had still to get used to the fact that there were so few westerners around, so few people of his own stature. He was, he now realized, part of a small and rapidly decreasing minority.

Being in a minority didn't bother him. Being very hot,

however, was extremely annoying. Especially as so many – western – people had already told him that now, November, was the sunniest, most temperate and least humid time of year. A Chinese associate had then informed him that November officially heralded the beginning of winter and that the weather, officially, was cold. To Fitz, both statements corroborated the opinion he had already formed: namely that Hong Kong was a crazy, contradictory and crass place. Give him Manchester any day.

Wiping the sweat off his forehead, he pushed his way through the swing-doors of the university building and, with a sigh of relief, entered the air-conditioned cool of the foyer. Like just about every other building in Hong Kong, it was almost brand new. History, it seemed, wasn't very important here. Everyone – especially now – was too concerned about what was going to happen tomorrow rather than what happened yesterday. Fitz thought that a prime example of crassness. History was important to him: vital to his profession. As a criminal psychologist, he regarded history – personal history, in particular – as the clue to human behaviour. It had been the subject of the first lecture he had given at Hong Kong University. And it was an essential component of today's lecture: subject, Negative and Positive Conditioning. Object, to make Hong Kong's third-year psychology undergraduates aware that they were being lectured by a genius.

Being invited to do a lecture tour of the Far East had rather gone to Fitz's head. Back home, his colleagues in

Manchester's CID had howled when they had heard the news. Fitz in the Philippines? Fitz in Singapore? In Hong Kong? Fitz on a giant freebie, more like.

Fitz was used to rubbing people up the wrong way. Mostly he did it deliberately; to get results. This time, however, he had made a good job of alienating everyone he had ever worked with. But then, maybe it had been time to move away – to move on. Since last year's catastrophic events, nothing and nobody had been the same at Anson Road Police Station. Sexual deviancy, rape and murder were, all too often, subjects to which Manchester's police devoted their lives. Sacrificing their lives to them was different. Soul-destroying. Shattering. Final. And Fitz's personal life had shattered at the same time. No; the circuit lecture in the Far East had come at the right time. Even if it was November in Hong Kong.

Fitz was scheduled to talk for an hour. An hour and a quarter after he began, he was still in full flood. He was also in full voice. To the consternation of his audience, he was singing. 'I hear the sound', he crooned into the microphone that he had snatched from the lectern, 'of distant drums; bu-bu-bu-bum, bu-bu-bu-bum.' Stamping his feet in time with his imaginary drums, he began, rock-star fashion, to pace the stage. His audience was now thoroughly alarmed. Most of them were well-educated Hong Kong Chinese and, as such, had paid polite, even eager, attention to the strange man prancing about in front of them. Their psychology lecturer had informed them that Dr Fitzgerald was an internationally respected criminal psychologist. They had therefore – and in spite of his broad, difficult Scottish accent – respectfully hung on to his every word. Some of those words had been peculiar in the extreme. And now the man was singing. The students exchanged covert, puzzled glances.

Suddenly Fitz had finished. With one last, dramatic thrust of the microphone, he stood and stared, half-triumphant and half-expectant, at his audience. More discreet, perplexed looks. Should they clap? Had he finished the lecture?

Fitz solved the problem for them. 'I'm singing that song', he boomed as he wiped a bead of perspiration off his forehead, 'and I've got the hairs coming up on the back of my neck.' He paused for a few, theatrical seconds. 'Why?'

None of the students knew why. Embarrassment, maybe?

'Because', said Fitz, before anyone ventured an answer, 'the only time my father whistled that tune was when he tried to control his temper.' He paused again and looked at the sea of blank faces. Then he smiled. 'My father never *did* control his temper, so 'Distant Drums' was always the prelude to a slap around the head. *That*', he added with something akin to venom, 'is negative conditioning.' He paused again, this time for a few more seconds, and then went back to stand behind the lectern. 'I'd claim now that it made me a better person,' he said in a calmer, more lecturer-like voice. Some of the students, unaware that they had been holding their breath, let out relieved, audible sighs. Fitz didn't have to hear the sighs to know of their existence. If there was one thing he knew, it was how to hold an audience. He smiled, eliciting, as he knew he would, smiles in response. 'It certainly made me a faster runner,' he said with a merry glint in his eye. The students grinned even more broadly. 'But', continued Fitz as he held up a finger, 'it *could* have been the perfect *trigger* for a pathological mind. Some killers rely on the smallest of excuses to commit the most heinous crimes. And whistling 'Distant Drums' is not small; it could have acted as a highly effective trigger. By rights,' he said with another smile, 'I should be barking mad and angry.'

The students grinned again. This was more like it; more the sort of thing they were used to. Then Fitz frightened the life out of them by leaping forward and roaring at the top of his voice. Everyone flinched as if they'd been hit. Then they assumed half-annoyed, half-sheepish expressions. Most of them felt a bit silly; the brighter of their number realized that Fitz *wanted* them to feel that way. The last thing Fitz wanted was for these people to go away thinking themselves superior. Fitz knew all about that sort of feeling.

Now smiling again, Fitz clasped his hands behind his back and inclined his head towards his audience. 'I thank you,' he said. Then, at first to tentative and then to rousing applause, he left the stage. Two members of his audience, however, hardly applauded at all. One of them, Freddie Cheung, was the university administrator who had the dubious honour of 'looking after' Fitz during his visit. The other, Freddie's sister Janet, was a senior policewoman. She had hoped to be enlightened by Fitz's lecture. Irritated was a more accurate description of her feelings as Fitz left the room. She reckoned she had learned nothing from him. She also reckoned that, were she to meet him, she wouldn't like him. Thank goodness, she told herself, that he was leaving in two days' time.

But Janet Lee Cheung should have remembered that the British had a habit of outstaying their welcome in Hong Kong.

Chapter One

Money. The powerful, all-absorbing love of gain. That's what it was all about. That was the point of 'The Pearl of the Orient'. Nobody, mused Dennis, called Hong Kong by that name any more – except travel agents who wanted only one thing, which was, of course, money.

Money. A tiny bead of sweat trickled down Dennis's forehead. It wasn't the heat that bothered him; it wasn't even that hot. A breezy, sunny day that people in England would call 'lovely' and then grumble about because it 'wouldn't last'. Or did they still say things like that? Dennis supposed they did. English people never changed, certainly not in the space of ten years. Dennis frowned and walked towards the window of his office. Here, in contrast, everything had changed over the last decade. The skyscrapers had all been knocked down

and rebuilt, only to be sold, pulled down again and to re-emerge in shimmering coats of glass and steel, screaming, even more loudly, 'look at me'.

The view from Dennis's office had altered dramatically within the last two years. Even the sea behind the buildings had retreated and been reclaimed by and for people who wanted to squeeze yet more money out of the teeming anthill of Hong Kong island. Where, thought Dennis, will it all end?

Another bead of sweat trickled down Dennis's pale brow. Endings. He didn't want to think about endings. Too close to the bone. But what else, he thought in sudden panic, is there to think about? Then, suddenly, a smile lit up his boyish features; a light shone in his deep blue eyes. What on earth was he being so maudlin about? Why contemplate Armageddon when creation was about to change his life? What on earth was he worrying about money for when something far more important, something *permanent*, was going to happen to him? The smile broadened. Dennis was happy once more.

Still smiling, he turned away from the window and looked at his watch. The order currently being processed on the factory floor below was urgent – and vitally important. He would go down to check that it would be out on time. He knew he didn't really have to: Jimmy, his frighteningly efficient Cantonese foreman, would have everything under control. His main reason for descending was nothing to do with business: he wanted his employees to share his happiness; he wanted to make the news public, to tell everyone that he and Su-Lin were expecting a baby. And he wanted to tell them when Su-Lin was there. He looked at his watch again. She would be going to see her mother in half an hour. Now was the time.

When he returned to his office ten minutes later, he was practically delirious with joy. It was almost, he thought with a grin, as if *he* were the pregnant one: his mood swings had been violent of late. Anger, sadness, ecstasy, worry and hope: his emotions dipped and rose like a barometer on speed. And Su-Lin, as ever, was so quiet, so sensible, so demure. When he had grabbed her by the elbow and pulled her into the middle of the factory floor and shouted their news to the assembled workers, she had bowed her head, modestly hiding her smile under her mane of long, dark hair.

Except that Su-Lin hadn't been smiling. Her expression, as Dennis had broadcast their news, had not been one of joy. It had been of fear.

Standing at his office window again, Dennis's own expression changed. Out of the corner of his eye, he saw a vast, chauffeur-driven Mercedes limousine glide into the forecourt below him. Peter. Peter never came here any more. If anything needed to be discussed, he sent a minion. Peter had a lot of minions. And recently, they had become irritatingly protective of their boss. Not even Dennis, a friend and business associate of several years' standing, had been able to get him on the phone. Dennis knew why. It had happened with other people.

It was because of money.

The intercom on his desk buzzed a few moments later. 'Yes?' he said in the quiet, accentless, yet slightly strained voice he had cultivated years ago. Shades of Romford, Essex, didn't do in Hong Kong. Estuary English, they would have called it. They would have called him FILTH behind his back; that damning acronym that meant Failed in London, Try Hong Kong.

'Mr Yang to see you,' replied his secretary. Her voice, precise and equally accentless, betrayed not the slightest hint of surprise at Peter Yang's unannounced visit. But then Fiona Chang was extremely adept at disguising how she felt. Only her eyes betrayed her inner feelings. Nowadays Dennis tried to avoid those eyes. Where he had once seen admiration, even deference, he now saw something akin to pity.

'Oh.' Dennis arranged a smile. 'Send him up, will you?' Then he looked around the office. It was, as usual, a mess. Peter Yang would notice. Peter would think that Dennis was letting things get out of hand. Peter would think . . .

Galvanized into action by sudden panic, Dennis started to scrabble at the piles of paper on his desk. He had succeeded in adding to, rather than clearing up, the mess when Fiona Chang knocked and, without waiting for a reply, ushered Peter Yang into the office.

'Mr Yang,' she announced unnecessarily. Then, lowering her eyes, she left the room. Dennis was under no illusions as to whom the deferential gesture was directed. In a country where 'face' was all-important, subordinates did their utmost to show their respect to their superiors. And very few people were superior to Peter Yang.

By dint of his own nationality and by their mutual friendship, Dennis Philby treated Peter Yang as an equal. Had he been a more perceptive individual, he would have been wise to show a little more deference to Peter Yang. Especially now that Peter was one of his few remaining clients. Philby Medical, suppliers of pharmaceuticals to major exporters, was not supplying anything very much at the moment.

'Peter,' said Dennis, stepping forward and pumping the older man's hand for rather longer than was necessary, 'I've been down at the loading bay, so . . .' Trailing off into silence, he gestured at the mound of papers on his desk. Then he looked up again. Peter Yang was not smiling. 'Er . . . tea?' he asked. The offer was born as much from desperation as from politeness.

Peter smiled his acceptance. The smile, Dennis noted as he buzzed Fiona Chang, was a trifle strained.

'I was beginning to wonder', he said as he waved Peter to a chair, 'whether you knew I still existed.' His tone was light-hearted, jocular even. Peter, elegant and immaculate in his expensive charcoal grey suit, smiled again. The smile failed to reach his eyes.

Dennis picked up a pen and began to fiddle with it. 'Nancy all right?' he asked. 'Not hiding?'

Neither of them knew what Nancy Yang was supposed to be hiding from. It was just something to say. Nancy was one of the territory's most prominent socialites.

'She's okay.'

'Kids all right?'

'Yes.'

'Good.' But Dennis couldn't bear it any longer. 'Er . . . what's up, Peter? You look worried.' And so, he thought, am I.

Peter reached into his breast pocket and extracted a sheet of newspaper. It was, Dennis saw, one of the major Chinese trade papers. Peter leaned forward and indicated a small article near the bottom of the page.

'Dennis, I want you to take a look at this.'

Dennis quelled a sudden panic. 'What's it say?' he asked with feigned nonchalance.

Peter's eyes bored into him. 'That you're in trouble.'

'Is that a question?'

Both of them knew it wasn't.

'Dennis,' sighed Peter, 'I need a better price on the order going through.' He looked, as did Dennis, towards the internal window overlooking the shop floor. He had seen his order being processed as he had walked through the building, parting the waves of the workers with nothing more than his presence.

Dennis snorted in derision. That was just silly. 'You're kidding me, Peter. How the hell can I do it for less?'

Peter Yang remained silent for a moment. Dennis, he knew, *couldn't* do it for less. Other people could, though. People on the mainland. People with lower overheads – and higher business acumen. 'You can't', he said quietly, 'afford not to.'

For a moment the two men just stared at each other. Dennis felt a queasy sensation in the pit of his stomach;

a vague premonition of fear ran down his spine. Peter remained inscrutable. Then, still with his eyes on Dennis, he reached into his breast pocket again and extracted another printed document. This one was pristine, the paper of good quality. And clearly visible at the top were the words 'Yang Associates'.

'It's a Contract of Sale,' said Peter, placing it on the desk between them. 'I'll buy you out.'

'*What?*'

'Whatever you owe, I'll cover it. Then you can go home.'

Go home? Buy me out? Dennis recoiled as if he had been hit. Then, disbelieving, he gestured at the internal window. 'All this? This factory for the price of my debts?'

Peter lowered his eyes. Didn't Dennis *know?* Wasn't he aware that everyone was talking, that people were falling over themselves in their stampede away from Philby Medical? He looked up again and saw, to his surprise, real hatred in Dennis's eyes.

'It's only worth', he said, echoing Dennis's gesture, 'what someone will pay for it.' And I, he could have added, am the only one who *is* willing. I'm only doing this to help an old friend. This, the one and only bad business decision of my life. Philby Medical wasn't even worth the price of its debts. Bad business decision or not, Peter Yang had, as usual, been diligent in his background research. He knew exactly how much Dennis owed.

The flash of hatred was fleeting: Dennis was now incredulous. And hurt. For a long moment he just glared at Peter. Then he found his voice. It was louder and higher than usual. And now it carried with it more than a hint of Estuary English. 'You've spent ten years watching me build up this business – and now you're poking *this*' – he stabbed at the contract – 'under my nose.'

Peter looked away.

'What's the problem, Peter?' Dennis's voice was suddenly sneering, almost mocking. 'Your Beijing buccaneers telling you not to play with me any more?'

Now it was Peter who looked as if he had been hit. Nobody told him what to do or how to do it. Nobody ever had – or would. Po-faced, he explained that to Dennis.

Dennis ignored him. 'So what about that lot down there?' What about Su-Lin? She's an integral part of the business. And she's pregnant. *We're* pregnant. We need to carry on, to ride out the storm. 'What are they supposed to do?'

Peter sighed and shook his head. He was prepared to do something for Dennis – but he wasn't a philanthropist. He was one of Hong Kong's most successful and hard-headed businessmen. He had a Rolls Royce and a Mercedes, a spacious house on the Peak and a villa at Sai Kung; bank accounts all over the world. And he hadn't achieved all that by propping up ailing businesses for the sake of a few blue-collar workers. They would find other work after he closed the factory. They would survive without help. But he wasn't so sure about Dennis. Again he met the Englishman's eye.

'Think about yourself now, Dennis.'

Dennis, eyes suddenly narrowed, was doing exactly

that. He snatched at the contract on the desk and screwed it into a tight little ball. Then he threw it at Peter.

'Get out!' he screamed.

Peter Yang stood up. Although shorter than Dennis, his innate air of authority more than compensated.

'Dennis,' he said in a quiet, kind voice, 'I'm offering you a way out.'

But Dennis had had enough. Nobody patronized Dennis Philby; least of all some jumped-up little Chink who had probably started life in the paddy fields.

'That', he yelled as he pointed at the door, 'is the way out!'

Peter Yang realized that now was not the time for rational debate. There would be another opportunity. After Dennis had calmed down, he would realize that the offer was sensible, not to say generous.

Yang shrugged and opened the door. If he was annoyed he didn't show it: his expression was as impassive and inscrutable as ever. Yet he was more disgusted than annoyed; more saddened than angry. That the once-proud Dennis Philby had degenerated into a pathetic, pitiable individual was tragic indeed. But life was full of tragedies. Chinese people knew that – and they knew the only way to deal with them was with stoicism.

Exiting the room, Yang narrowly avoided colliding with Fiona Chang. Both of them, taken by surprise, uttered profuse apologies. Steadying the tea-tray in her hands, Fiona looked behind Peter to Dennis's office. Her

15

boss, red in the face and perspiring freely, was breathing deeply, seemingly fighting to control himself. Forgetting for a moment who Peter Yang was, Fiona looked at him, eyebrows raised in silent inquisition. Peter smiled sadly, shook his head and made his way towards the stairwell. The secretary, he thought to himself, knew, as secretaries often did, exactly what was going on. She knew that Dennis Philby was cracking up; that it was only a matter of time before he lost his increasingly tenuous grip on reality.

At the same time as Peter Yang was reclining in the back of his chauffeur-driven Mercedes *en route* to more pleasing locations than Philby Medical, Fitz had left the university lecture-hall and was firmly ensconced in a location that, in the normal scheme of things, should have been extremely pleasing to him. He was in a bar. Yet this was no normal bar: it was the university bar and it was dry. Fitz had discovered that after his previous lecture. Never easily thwarted, he had decided to solve the problem by arming himself on this occasion with a whisky-filled hip flask.

'Just ice,' he said to the barman as he leaned over the counter. The barman, unaccustomed to people 'drinking' neat ice, was trying to pour water into the glass in front of Fitz. 'No!' Fitz held up a hand. 'Just *ice!*' The barman shrugged. Fitz turned to back to his companion.

'So, you think it lost something in the translation?'

Freddie Cheung, who didn't know Fitz very well, had dared to criticize, albeit mildly, his lecture.

'All I was saying,' he began, 'is that perhaps . . .'

' . . . Well bloody *tough*!' snapped Fitz.

Freddie recoiled in horror. Then he saw that the other man was grinning.

'Freud', continued Fitz as he extracted the hip flask from his pocket, 'didn't make sense for forty years. Laing', he added as he poured a hefty slug into the ice-filled glass, 'still doesn't.'

'Mmm.' Freddie stroked his chin and eyed Fitz with interest. The man, he thought, made absolutely no concessions; he didn't seem to care if he caused offence with his brash behaviour. In a way, Freddie rather admired him for it. And despite the brashness, he rather liked Fitz as a person. He had guts. And attack, he decided, was the best form of defence against him.

'Most English-speaking circuit lecturers', he began with a slight smile, 'try to modify their behaviour for clarity.'

Fitz took a giant swig of his drink and eyed Freddie with suspicion. Another criticism. He rather liked that. Then he put his glass down, refilled it and glared at Freddie.

'I'd just do the song,' he said, 'if it didn't affect the money.' Then he shrugged and returned the smile. 'I'd do it in a frock if it didn't affect the money.'

Freddie noted the smile; but the woman who had edged up to them and who was now standing behind Fitz did not. She heard only the words, and the dismissive tone in which they were spoken.

'Arrogant bastard,' she half-whispered.

Fitz whirled round to see a slight, pretty Chinese woman with intelligent eyes and an unmistakable air of authority. He suspected, although he couldn't be sure, that she had just called him an arrogant bastard. He looked through, rather than at her.

'Pardon me?' he said.

The woman ignored him. She turned to Freddie and spoke again, this time in Cantonese.

'So this is you improving the lecture stock?' Her body language made it abundantly clear that she was referring, not altogether kindly, to Fitz.

Freddie grinned. 'He comes highly recommended,' he replied in the same language. 'Just takes some warming up. Apparently.'

Fitz was getting annoyed. 'My ears', he said in the only language he knew, 'are burning.'

The woman looked at him with scorn. 'It's a shame your arse isn't,' she drawled in an accent that, like Freddie's, was pure Ivy League.

Fitz looked to Freddie for enlightenment. 'What did she say?'

Freddie did his best to suppress his grin. 'Oh . . . just that she, er . . . enjoyed the lecture.'

As he spoke, the woman stalked off the rejoin her companions at the other end of the bar. Fitz, frowning, watched her retreating back. Arrogant bitch, he thought. Then Freddie, to his astonishment, announced that the woman was his sister.

'Your sister?' Again he whirled round.

'Yes. My sister Janet. She's a policewoman.'

'A policewoman?'

Freddie grinned. 'Yes. A policewoman. There's a lot of police here, you know. Your reputation precedes you.'

Fitz was still contemplating whether he had been complimented or insulted when they were interrupted, this time loudly, by a tall, greyish-blond Englishman sporting an unflattering and unfashionable moustache. He beamed broadly at Fitz.

'Dr Fitzgerald?' he asked in plummy tones as he held out a hand. 'May I say what a bloody corking lecture that was?'

Fitz shot Freddie a triumphant look.

'Clear as a bell,' continued the newcomer as he pumped Fitz's hand with vigour. 'Well done. Well done!'

Fitz smiled up at him; a question implicit in the gesture.

'Ah!' The answer came without further prompting. 'Commander Gordon Ellison. Royal Hong Kong Police Force.' Then Ellison's smile faded somewhat as he noticed the amber liquid in Fitz's glass. 'You know this is a dry bar, by the way?'

Fitz didn't miss a beat. 'This is mouth-wash,' he replied as he drained the contents of the glass.

Ellison roared with laughter and clapped him on the shoulder.

'Come on,' he said. 'Follow me. I think you'd be happier somewhere more . . . more *European*.' Then he turned to Freddie. 'You'll come with us?'

Freddie nodded and stood up. 'Delighted.' Commander Ellison was his sister's boss. It would be an enlightening experience to have drinks with him. According to Janet, he epitomized all that was worst about *gweilos*. She had said he was an expat of the old school; a colonial living in a different age – and that he was marking time until his retirement in May. But she only ever said these things to people outside the police force – Janet Lee Cheung was tipped to take his place when he left Hong Kong.

It was just as well, then, that Ellison failed to notice Janet as he led Fitz and Freddie out of the bar. Had he done so, he would undoubtedly have asked her to join them. And Janet had revised the opinion she had formed of Fitz during his lecture. The dislike she had anticipated had changed to disgust.

Ellison, however, was delighted to have the chance to entertain a newcomer: to 'show him the sights'. Hailing one of the ubiquitous red and white taxis, he instructed the driver to take them to Admiralty.

'There's a bar', he said to Fitz as they climbed into the vehicle, 'that'll remind you of home.' Fitz didn't notice the wry grin on Freddie's face as Ellison spoke. Ellison himself seemed blissfully unaware, as he settled himself into the front seat of the taxi, that 'home' for Fitz might be rather different from his own romantic visions of Merrie England.

Fitz lapsed into an uncustomary silence during the journey. As he looked around, he reflected on the incongruity of Ellison's words. How on earth could any part of Hong Kong remind him of home? The teeming crowds;

the towering skyscrapers; the impossibly cramped living conditions; the washing hanging out of every apartment-block window and the never-ending building noises as yet more buildings were constructed – Manchester had absolutely nothing in common with this place. Edinburgh, his childhood home, had even less.

Fitz looked out of the window and shook his head. Hong Kong, he decided, would get on his nerves if he had to stay here much longer. Then the taxi braked sharply and, as the driver erupted with a volley of outraged Cantonese and every vehicle in sight started tooting, Fitz turned to Freddie. The man seemed completely unperturbed by the cacophony around them.

'Wouldn't we be better off walking?' he asked. Coming from Fitz, this was a most unusual statement.

Freddie looked extremely surprised. 'Walking? Why?'

Fitz indicated the stationary traffic. Freddie looked blank.

'The traffic,' sighed Fitz. 'We're not going anywhere.'

Freddie waved a dismissive hand. Then he looked at his watch. It was six o'clock. 'Rush hour,' he said.

Fitz looked gloomy. It always seemed to be rush hour in Hong Kong. 'Christ!' he said as he gestured at the gridlock. 'I've just finished a lecture about conditioning. What sort of conditioning is *this*? A trigger for road rage? Incitement to murder?'

Freddie was looking not a little puzzled. He couldn't see what Fitz was making such a fuss about.

'Oh no,' he replied. 'People are pretty law-abiding here. It's one of the nice things about Hong Kong.'

Fitz shot him a suspicious, sideways glance. *One* of the nice things? Were there others, then?

'Murders', continued Freddie, 'are relatively uncommon in Hong Kong.'

'Oh?' Fitz didn't believe a word of it.

Freddie noted the expression. 'Unless', he corrected, 'you count organized crime. Triad killings, that sort of thing. They can be pretty brutal,' he finished in a matter-of-fact tone. Then he looked back at Fitz, scowling and sweating beside him. 'You may think otherwise, but it takes a lot more than a spot of traffic to incite a Hong Kong citizen to murder.'

'Huh.' Fitz looked out of the window again.

Ellison, who had missed the conversation in the back seat because of the din around them, suddenly turned round. 'The bar I'm taking you to', he said with a smile, 'has a happy hour from five till eight.'

Fitz cheered up. A three-hour happy hour, he supposed, was some compensation for a permanent rush hour.

Despite the traffic, it was still happy hour when they reached the Royal Oak. But then, reflected Fitz as Ellison ordered their drinks, the establishment needed all the happiness it could get. The place looked as if it were a Sino-American vision – realized, probably, by the Japanese – of old England. It stopped short – just – of serving wenches. Otherwise it was a riot of imitation ale casks, oak beams, 'antiques', panelled walls and padded chintz chairs.

Having given their order to the Australian waitress, Ellison turned to Fitz. He was, once more, beaming delightedly.

'While you're in Hong Kong,' he said kindly, 'mention my name at the door when you come here. They'll always find you a table.'

Not trusting himself to reply, Fitz gave Ellison an appreciative smile. Then he cast what he hoped was an admiring glance at the other patrons of the Royal Oak. Most of them, grey-suited and serious, could have been English businessmen. Most of them, Fitz noted with a start, *were* English businessman. Or boys. The average age seemed to be about twenty-five. Their talk was sub-dued – due mainly to the fact that many of them, rather than talking to each other, were mumbling into their mobile phones. Others, waiting for wives, girlfriends or colleagues, were staring moodily around. They looked disconcerted by the atmosphere. Or maybe, thought Fitz as the waitress arrived with their drinks, they were put out by the Taiwanese piped music (Elgar?) tinkling in the background. Fitz turned back to his companions, carefully avoiding Freddie's eye. Then he picked up his glass and saluted Gordon Ellison. A complete change of subject, he reckoned, was called for.

'What's the accent, Gordon?' he asked with a smile. 'Scotland Yard?'

'Cheers!' Ellison raised his own glass. 'Cheltenham, actually,' he replied. He didn't appear to be aware that Fitz's question was more than a little tongue-in-cheek. His accent, the clipped vowels and nasal drawl, was all pink gin and polo. Then he leaned conspiratorially towards Fitz.

'You wouldn't believe how I ended up in the police force.'

No, thought Fitz, I probably wouldn't.

'When I got off the boat,' continued the older man as he sipped his gin and tonic, 'I was a primary-school headmaster.' With that, he burst out laughing. Fitz smiled dutifully. Freddie buried his face in his drink. He knew, via Janet, all about Ellison's past. And he knew that Ellison had a reputation for boring people to death with anecdotes about his schoolteaching days.

'You wouldn't believe', began Ellison as soon as he stopped laughing, 'the story about the French teacher and . . . bugger!' Fitz stared, surprised, at the ex-headmaster. The punchline seemed to have arrived before the joke. Then he noted that the last word was directed at the bleeper Ellison was now fishing out of his jacket pocket. Ellison shot him a look that was both annoyed and embarrassed.

'Sorry,' he said as he silenced the offending object. 'Bleeper.'

Then he looked at the message on the tiny screen and, even more annoyed, rolled his eyes. 'I'm very sorry about this,' he said, with genuine regret, as he stood up. Fitz suspected, correctly, that the regret was more for the anecdote than for his companions.

'You must', he said to Fitz as he pushed back his chair, 'come round for dinner.' Another bellow of laughter. 'Try and psychoanalyse my family, eh?'

That, thought Fitz, would be extremely interesting.

Then, remembering Freddie's existence, Ellison included him in his next remark. 'Stay as long as you want to,' he said with a gracious smile. 'Really.' Then he was gone.

Fitz waited a few moments and, much more eloquently than Ellison had done, rolled his eyes. Then he looked at their expat fellow-drinkers and finished his own drink in one gulp.

'Come on Freddie. If this is the "Spiritual Subtext" of the bloody Orient, I'm a Chinaman.'

Freddie laughed and stood up. 'You want to see what it's really all about, then?'

Fitz nodded. 'I'm all yours.'

Dennis Philby knew what it was all about. He knew all about the real Hong Kong and how the majority of the population lived. Whole families lived in two-room apartments; they kept ducks and chickens in their bathrooms; many of them lived 'above the shop' and sometimes the division between home and shop was theoretical rather than real. People lived to work *and* worked to live: the two words were synonymous.

And the most extraordinary thing, thought Dennis as he left his office at the same time as Ellison's party left the university, was that families like that weren't even considered poor: they wouldn't even consider themselves poor. Su-Lin's family lived like that – and they weren't poor. No doubt they considered themselves, he thought with sudden savagery, to be fortunate: rich in happiness and family life. Family life. Oh, thought Dennis, I knew all about that. That's why I came here: both to escape and re-create it. And I've done neither.

The car in front of Dennis, a taxi, suddenly stopped dead, forcing Dennis to slam on his own brakes.

'Bastards!' he yelled. Normally the traffic didn't bother him. But today everything bothered him. Everything enraged him. In an attempt to let off steam, he leaned on the horn. In the car in front, one of the passengers in the back seat turned round. A fat, pallid, dark-haired westerner, he glared in irritation at Dennis. Dennis glared back. At least, he thought with a bitter smile, I'm not in *that* bad shape. He looked down at his taut stomach and ran a hand through his thick, blond hair. Dennis was very careful with his hair; careful to keep it looking natural. Few people – and nobody in Hong Kong – knew that it was naturally dark. Then, suddenly annoyed at himself, he hit the horn again.

Not long ago, he reflected, he had been rich as well as attractive. Young, wealthy, blond and blue-eyed. He had had no difficulty attracting girls, Chinese girls especially – and Su-Lin in particular.

Dennis narrowed his eyes. Did Su-Lin know? Had she any idea about what was happening with the business? He doubted it: he had been scrupulous about keeping things from her – especially now.

He hooted again. Stupid fat people, he thought. Why can't they get out and walk? They were probably only going to the Hong Kong Club anyway. Or for drinks at the Mandarin. Places so near you could throw stones at

26

them. Places that Dennis could only dream about. He, he thought savagely, was going to the real Hong Kong: to Su-Lin's parents' mini-market in Shau Kei Wan, the most dismal concrete jungle on the island. Acres of apartment blocks and not a rich *gweilo*'s playground in sight.

By the time Dennis reached Su-Lin's family's mini-market, four miles and half an hour later, his mood had changed again. Now he felt elated; almost manic. He parked the car, illegally, and walked into the small, crowded shop. Su-Lin's cousin, Mei Ming, was minding the counter at the back. She smiled broadly as she saw Dennis – 'blue eyes' – walking into the shop. The whole extended family was very fond of Dennis. Despite the fact that his visits were both short and infrequent, they were, nevertheless, visits from a rich, generous *gweilo*. And, according to Su-Lin who knew about these things, he was considered very good-looking. The rest of the family couldn't quite see it for themselves, but they were prepared to believe her. They were also – with less conviction – prepared to believe that he was going to ask her to marry him. 'Soon', according to Su-Lin. 'Soon' was a term that had been bandied about for some time now.

Dennis nodded to Mei Ming as he came up to her. She had little English; he had but a smattering of Cantonese and they communicated, perforce, through a series of nods and smiles. Mei Ming greeted his nod with a broad smile and a raised hand. The hand meant that Su-Lin was upstairs with the rest of the family. Dennis climbed the steep staircase at the back of the shop. His spirits sank again. The stairway was crowded with supplies;

boxes of washing powder, of pot noodles, of freeze-dried delicacies and fish-food littered the narrow area. The apartment above, he knew, would be exactly the same. With space at a premium, there was nowhere else to store the goods sold at the mini-market. It was all such a horrible contrast to Dennis's spacious apartment. He still couldn't understand why Su-Lin spent so much time here.

He turned the corner and entered the main room of the apartment. Compact in the first place, it was made smaller by its contents. More boxes vied for space with two tables, a giant colour television set, several chairs, a vast, intricately carved birdcage with three multi-coloured occupants and assorted paraphernalia of everyday Chinese family life. Again, a stark contrast to Dennis's sleek, minimalist home in Happy Valley. He frowned as he surveyed the scene. The television was blaring; the birds were chirping and four of the people in the room were chattering in loud, rapid-fire Cantonese. Dennis didn't like loud noise. It upset him.

But the expression on Su-Lin's face when she looked up and saw him standing there made up for everything. Even after five years, Dennis's heart still sometimes missed a beat when he studied her exquisite features. She was beautiful. Their child, too, would be beautiful.

Su-Lin rose from the sofa. 'You're early.'

'I know.' Dennis forced a smile. 'I missed you.' Well, it was partly true. Why hang around at work with nothing to do when he could be with his girlfriend? But not here. He had to get out of here.

'Blue eyes!' This, in Cantonese, from Su-Lin's mother Wei Wei. Her lined face crinkled even more as she smiled at her prospective son-in-law. Marriage would happen soon. Then Su-Lin would have a baby. That's what would happen. She patted the space beside her on the sofa. Su-Lin's father, although engrossed as usual in a Chinese soap opera on TV, also flashed a ready smile at Dennis. The two other people in the room, friends of Su-Lin, blushed a delicate shade of pink. Dennis felt even more uncomfortable. Who did they think he was: a performing dog? He looked to Su-Lin. She recognized the 'let's go' expression in his eyes. For a fleeting moment, disappointment registered in her own dark eyes. Then the shutters came down.

She turned back to the three women.

'We're going to go,' she said in her native language. 'Dennis', she added with a wicked smile, 'is missing me.' The others nodded. If Dennis wanted her to go, then go she must. Her mother hid her disappointment. Su-Lin's visits were becoming more infrequent: Dennis's even rarer.

Then her daughter bent down to the list the women had been compiling; a list of guests for her father's forthcoming birthday party. The Tang family took birthdays extremely seriously.

'Don't forget to post them tomorrow,' she said. 'And don't', she added with a grin, 'forget the Changs!' Then she picked up her handbag and, with a last wave, accompanied Dennis out of the room.

Wei Wei stared after her. Despite Su-Lin's breezy cheerfulness, her mother knew intuitively that something was wrong. She had known the minute Su-Lin had arrived earlier in the day. She had been too upbeat. Yet, as usual, she confided nothing. Her relationship with Dennis was 'fine' and the business was 'going well'. She and Dennis had enjoyed their holiday. Dennis had bought her two new dresses. Wasn't she spoiled? There was no other news.

Wei Wei had not been convinced. There was something wrong. Her daughter's relationship with Dennis had always been up and down – Dennis was an extremely volatile man – but this time there was something seriously amiss. And if Su-Lin's attitude had aroused her suspicions, Dennis's face had confirmed them. Dennis might be rich, generous and kind – but he was a weak man. Wei Wei knew all about weak men. She cast a surreptitious glance at her husband and then, determinedly cheerful, rejoined Su-Lin's friends in writing the party invitations. Her daughter's life was too complicated for her; her relationship with Dennis even more so. Why weren't they like normal people? Why didn't they behave normally? Why on earth didn't they settle down properly, get married, and have children?

Su-Lin settled herself into the passenger seat of the BMW and turned to smile at Dennis. His hair, she noticed, was ruffled. Dennis was normally most particular about his hair – he even, to her amusement, went to great lengths to hide the dye he used. But now Dennis himself, despite his own determined smile, was more ruffled than his hair. He would tell her in time what was wrong. She knew better than to ask.

'Good day?' she enquired instead.

Dennis grimaced. 'I've had better.' Mustn't tell her, he thought. Not now. Not ever. Then, attempting to lighten the mood, he glanced down at Su-Lin's stomach and smiled.

Su-Lin didn't smile back.

'Let's chuck some money,' he said as he threw the car into gear. 'Have a meal out, eh? Somewhere in Lan Kwai Fong?'

A tiny frown creased Su-Lin's forehead. She hated Lan Kwai Fong. Full of expensive bars and restaurants – and of loud *gweilos*. The last, defiant outpost of a dying empire. 'No,' she said more vehemently than she meant. 'Not out. Let me cook.' She patted her stomach. She felt sick. 'I'll cook.'

'Okay.' Dennis merely shrugged, yet the rigidity in his shoulders as he pulled out into the traffic betrayed an inner tension. Su-Lin looked at him out of the corner of her eye, catching him in profile. He's aged, she thought, surprising herself with the realization. He looks tired and worn. Stressed. For the umpteenth time, she wished that Dennis didn't withdraw so completely into himself when something was wrong in that complex mind of his; wished that he wouldn't exclude her. She used to put up with it; stoically accepting the situation. But not now. She had had enough. She wanted her life back. It would ultimately be for the best; for his good as well as her own. What she had done yesterday, she thought as she put a tentative hand to her stomach, was for him as well as

31

her. The only thing was, she could never tell him about it. It would probably send him over the edge.

At the same time as Dennis and Su-Lin were travelling south to Happy Valley, Fitz and Freddie Cheung were heading in the opposite direction – by boat. The 'real' Hong Kong, according to Freddie, lay across the water from the island itself, on the Kowloon peninsula. And the traditional way to get there was on the Star Ferry.

'The Star Ferry?' Fitz shot Freddie a dubious look as they walked through the crowds towards the harbour-front.

'Yes. You know; those green and white boats that you see all the time.'

Fitz nodded. He wasn't about to tell Freddie that no, he hadn't seen them. And he certainly wasn't going to tell him that he tried to avoid boats at all costs. And heights. He hated heights; a phobia that was by necessity curing itself in Hong Kong.

Freddie was grinning as he led Fitz to the Star Ferry terminal. 'We'll travel second class,' he said. 'See how the other half live. Anyway, it's cheaper. Costs your equivalent of about ten pence.'

Oh well, thought Fitz, I suppose that's something. Hong Kong, thus far, had been staggeringly expensive. The price of booze was astronomical. If he was going to be sick on a boat, at least he wouldn't be paying through the nose for the pleasure.

He wasn't sick. He was jostled; pushed from side to side as a seemingly endless stream of Chinese joined them on the lower deck of the ferry. As usual, everyone was talking at the tops of their voices, screaming at each other in their strangely guttural language. And again as usual, the chatter was punctuated, by males and females alike, with throat clearing noises, with the hawking and spitting that Fitz had discovered to be the least attractive trait of the Chinese. How, he thought for the umpteenth time, can people ever get used to the crowds, the incessant noise, the frenetic and never-ceasing activity? Why weren't they all driven insane? He recalled Freddie's words about murder in Hong Kong. He didn't believe that killings were limited to organized crime. He envisaged that death was all around him – the deaths of people who 'didn't matter'; of illegal immigrants from China and elsewhere; of people living well below the poverty line; of people who didn't interest the police.

Pushing his way through the throng to the side of the boat, he stared out of the window. This was the busiest harbour in the world, he had been told – and he could well believe it. Even though it was now dark, the water was still buzzing with activity. There were boats everywhere. Tiny ill-lit sampans bobbed about, vying for space with larger junks. Flat-bottomed container vessels stood serene in the distance and, on the Kowloon side, two huge majestic cruise liners dwarfed the quayside. Everywhere Fitz looked there were boats. How, he wondered, could anybody possibly monitor what was happening here? How much smuggling was happening right under his very nose: how many poor deluded souls were coming here – legitimately and illegally – in their search for El Dorado? What secrets did the water hold? A shrine to modernity this place may be, thought Fitz, but there was something darkly Dickensian about it as well. Everything, in Hong Kong, appeared to be laid out for all to see: privacy seemed an alien concept. Yet the psychologist in him knew that behind the façade there would lurk the usual morass of ills: underneath the 'what you see is what you get' attitude of the citizens of Hong Kong, there would be danger and desperation, hope, love, despair, joy and madness. And Fitz, rather to his regret, would see none of it.

The journey took a mere seven minutes. Most of Fitz's fellow passengers were a foot shorter than he was; a fact that made little difference to them as they barged past him in their haste to disembark; to get home or to get to a bar; to start the next stage of whatever journey they were making; to go shopping or to get a haircut. To do anything as long as it was *something* in this city that never seemed to stop.

Fitz was in no doubt as to what he wanted to do most. He was parched.

'Well?' he said to Freddie as they reached terra firma. 'Where to? Where's this real Hong Kong of yours?'

Freddie laughed. 'Patience, Fitz. Something, since we're in this part of the world, that Confucius used to preach.'

'Something', said Fitz as he was nearly knocked off his feet by a swarm of chattering Cantonese, 'that they seem to have forgotten around here.'

Again Freddie laughed. For all his worldly wisdom,

Fitz seemed like a fish out of water here. The label 'tourist' sat uneasily on the hotshot criminal psychologist. Freddie suspected, correctly, that Fitz was something of a control freak. Observation and manipulation were his methods – and here he could only observe.

'Come on,' he said. 'The bar's only five minutes away.'

The five-minute walk was enough to tell Fitz why westerners preferred to live on Hong Kong island rather than in Kowloon. The crowds here were even worse; the traffic was terrible. And the riot of neon signs even more garish than on the island.

'If we have time,' mused Freddie, 'I can show you the most crowded place on earth.'

Fitz was horrified. 'You mean it gets *worse*?'

'Mmm. Mongkok', said Freddie, gesturing to the north, 'is unbelievable. More people per square mile than anywhere else in the world. More brothels, too. And', he added with a smile, 'more abortionists.'

'Well, that makes sense, I suppose.' Fitz decided he was damned if he was going anywhere near Mongkok. This area was quite enough.

'This area', continued Freddie as they turned into a seedy side-street, 'is Tsim Sha Tsui. Good for shopping. Lots of bargains.'

'Oh.' Fitz looked around without interest. The only thing he wanted to buy was alcohol. And soon. Gambling, he knew, was out: illegal in Hong Kong except at the races. Stupid law. Gambling was gambling, wasn't it?

'You mentioned gambling the other day,' said Freddie,

35

as if reading his mind. 'No casinos or anything, I'm afraid. Only allowed at the racetracks. Of course,' he continued, spiralling Fitz into a depression, 'the Chinese gamble illegally all over the place, but not your lot.'.

'Huh.'

Freddie grinned. Then, half-way down the street, he stopped and gestured towards a doorway. 'Here we go.' Pausing, as if having second thoughts, he shot his companion a look that was at once apologetic and admonitory. 'And, er . . . Fitz?'

'Yes?'

'Leave the talking to me, okay?'

Fitz shrugged. That was fine by him.

His presence, however, wasn't fine in the book of the bouncers who suddenly materialized as they went through the doorway. They glared at Fitz and then looked suspiciously at Freddie. 'It's all right,' said the latter in Cantonese, 'he's with me.'

The larger of the two bouncers – a good six inches shorter than Fitz but infinitely more threatening – unwillingly let them past. *Gweilos* were not welcome here: had Freddie not been a regular, they would have ejected them both.

Freddie led Fitz down the short staircase into the bowels of the building. The large room in which they found themselves was packed. Smoke filled the air; excited, high-pitched chatter assailed Fitz's ears. The air-conditioning either didn't exist or didn't work. For a moment Fitz stood still, trying to accustom himself to the din, the smell of sweat and the suggestion of vice in

36

the air. This, then, was it. A drinker's paradise. An illegal gambling den? A haven for Fitz.

All eyes, however, were on the western newcomer. The shouting stopped. And then people looked, questioning and suspicious, at Freddie. As he had done with the bouncers, he said a few conciliatory words in his native language. They were greeted with shrugs, with grunts of reluctant acceptance. Then the gambling resumed, the air was once again filled with excited chatter, with the snap of speedily dealt cards, the clatter of Mah Jong pieces. Freddie breathed a sigh of relief. Perhaps this hadn't been such a good idea after all. He had forgotten how threatening Fitz looked. And he suddenly remembered Fitz's arrogance, his refusal to make concessions of any kind. Grabbing him by the arm, he dragged him to the bar. A few drinks and then they would go. Half an hour of observation, of drinking in the atmosphere and then he would take him somewhere else.

Fitz, however, had other ideas. Grinning, he accepted a drink from the barman and, with a nod towards the card game in front of them, turned to Freddie.

'I think', he said, 'I've just found a pulse!'

Freddie shook his head. 'That's a private game. You're not invited.'

But Fitz waved that one aside. Gambling was the same the world over. And gamblers liked other gamblers. For the first time since he had arrived in Hong Kong, Fitz felt at home. He extracted his wallet from his rumpled jacket.

'You don't bet then, Freddie?' he said with a tinge of pity.

'No. And do you know what they call a *gweilo* with money?'

'A what?' Fitz frowned at the unfamiliar word.

'A *gweilo*. It's what the Cantonese call westerners. It means "white ghost".'

'Oh. So what do they call a white ghost with money?'

Freddie looked grim. 'The target.'

Fitz burst out laughing. Then he peeled a few notes from his wallet.

'And do you know what we call a man who never bets, Freddie?'

Freddie shook his head.

'The deceased.'

Then Fitz approached the gamblers, pulled out a chair from a nearby table and looked expectantly at the four card players. A horrified Freddie followed him.

'Fitz . . .' he began as he clocked the gamblers' murderous expressions.

'No,' said Fitz, shaking off his restraining hand. 'It's fine, really.' Then he smiled at the men in front of him and waved his wad of cash. 'I'm a tourist. I've got money to throw away.'

Freddie rolled his eyes. Then, stepping in front of Fitz, he started to jabber furiously at the four men at the table. His companion, he explained, would like to join them for a moment. He would be honoured if they would allow him to do so. He was offering them drinks. He would be no trouble.

The men looked at one another. Then the oldest of the four shrugged. A *gweilo* with money was, after all, an easy target. He gestured for Fitz to join them.

Fitz beamed from ear to ear. This was what it was all about. This was the life. He smiled at Freddie and sat down. Money was what counted in Hong Kong. And he intended to be counting a lot of money before the night was out. He would be a lucky white ghost.

Each consumed with their private worries, Dennis and Su-Lin travelled the rest of the way home in strained silence. Reaching Happy Valley, Dennis turned the car into the broad thoroughfare of Wong Nai Chong Road and accelerated. The sight of the racetrack on his right did little to cheer him up. People like Peter Yang, members of the exclusive Hong Kong Jockey Club, bet fortunes there on race nights. Millions of dollars exchanged hands on every race: half the unlucky punters not even missing the money. Dennis pursed his lips, remembering the not-so-distant days when he, too, would bet hefty sums. More than he could afford – but then one had to keep up appearances.

Five minutes later he was reminded of something else he couldn't afford; the spacious penthouse apartment off Bluepool Road. Su-Lin had stared, open-mouthed, when he had shown it to her two years ago. 'But it's *enormous*!' she had gasped, laughing because she didn't know what else to do. It *was* enormous; the rent was astronomical, and they spent a small fortune jetting off to Macau to buy antique furnishings. Yet, to Dennis, it had been worth it. The previous apartment had been in Sheung Wan – not nearly smart enough. Happy Valley or Mid-Levels were the 'right' enclaves for the English. No traces of Romford there – and if there were, they had been carefully painted over with a veneer of sophistication. The veneer that permeated the entire territory of Hong Kong.

The amah, as usual, had left the apartment immaculate. Dennis had wanted her to live in, to occupy the squalid 'room' behind the kitchen. Su-Lin had put her foot down. A live-in amah meant a resident cook – and Su-Lin loved cooking, couldn't stand anyone else in her kitchen. The arrangement suited Nerita down to the ground. It meant she could take on an evening job – and live with her sister in the room behind the kitchen of another rich person's apartment.

It was to the kitchen that Su-Lin repaired as soon as they reached the apartment. Cooking was her therapy; it would instil in her a calmness, a confidence to tackle Dennis. And food would mellow him; soften the blow she would deliver. Dennis himself, as was his way, headed straight for the shower. Five minutes later, he came back into the large, airy drawing-room, poured himself a hefty gin and tonic and ambled onto the balcony.

It was night now, dusk had descended with its usual briskness – but Hong Kong wasn't dark. Dennis liked that; he relished the fact that the sunset heralded a blaze of neon, that here in the centre of the city, darkness never descended. The streets and buildings below were a kaleidoscope of colour. Above and around him, lights flashed continuously; lights in the high-rise blocks of Mid-Levels that clung precariously to the hillside; lights on the more distant Peak announcing that the very rich were happily ensconced in their very expensive homes. The thought annoyed Dennis. He took a hefty slug of his drink. Peter Yang lived there. Peter bloody Yang, his wife, children and his fleet of servants. Would he be there now, looking down from his terrace, surveying the lesser mortals below? No, thought Dennis, not Peter. He would still be at work. Generating even more money. Dennis drained his drink and walked back into the drawing-room. It was, like the streets below, bathed in light. Dennis made a point of switching on all the lights as soon as he entered the apartment. All of them. Su-Lin had at first tried to remonstrate with him, pointing out what a terrible waste of money it was. She had been surprised and not a little shocked by the vehemence of his response. He hated the dark, he had said. Couldn't bear dark rooms. He had to have light. Su-Lin had shrugged and dismissed it as just another of his little quirks.

But now Su-Lin was seriously alarmed by his increasing quirkiness, by the violence of his mood swings. Putting the finishing touches to the food as Dennis poured himself another drink, she steeled herself to say what she knew she must.

But Dennis was steeling himself for his own bombshell. He dispatched his second gin and tonic in a matter of seconds and, as Su-Lin emerged from the kitchen carrying a bowl of steaming rice, was opening a bottle of wine. When she returned with the pak choi and the chicken, he had already downed half a glass.

She couldn't stand it any longer. 'Dennis . . . ?' she prompted as she sat down.

Dennis drained his glass and reached for the bottle. 'Peter Yang wants to take the factory off me. He came round today and he was standing this distance from me' – he jabbed angrily at the bottle – 'and I'm still trying to work out why I didn't chin the bastard.'

Su-Lin was so stunned she couldn't speak. Stunned by what he had said – and by how he had said it. The rapidity of his delivery; the way the words had burst forth, shocked her. But more alarming was the deadpan voice, belying the import of the words. And now he was staring at her through blank eyes.

'I'm sorry,' he continued, still in the flat voice. 'I've let you down. I've let you down, I said.' He nodded to himself. 'I've kept it from you. I'm saying it now.'

'Saying what?' Su-Lin's head was spinning.

'I lost three big contracts between March and May. So I took a flyer and I accepted an order that I couldn't supply. And . . . and I hadn't the money to pay them back.' At last he betrayed a flicker of emotion, of shame. 'And now the bank is moving in. They want me . . . us, out of here.' Then, relieved, he poured another glass and downed it in one.

Su-Lin continued to stare. Nothing could have prepared her for this. Not her imagination; not her suspicions that something was amiss. For a moment, anger overtook her. Why hadn't he *said*? Why hadn't he confided in her? God knows, they both knew her brain, as well as his, was behind the business. Then she bit back the response that had sprung to her lips. That was part of the problem: her brain was better than his.

She looked at Dennis across the table, through the gentle spiral of steam from the rice – the only thing that was moving in the room. Her mind, now, was a blank. She knew she had to say something, there were so many things she *wanted* to say – yet the words eluded her.

Dennis suddenly threw his napkin across the table, leaped up from the table and marched to the 'living' side of the huge room. He stopped in front of an antique rosewood armoire, wrenched open the door, and pulled an old holdall from the bottom shelf. Then, with an angry look at Su-Lin's hesitant progress towards him, he threw open the bag.

'Look!' he spat, gesturing at the contents.

Still silent, Su-Lin bent down towards the bag. Her mind was still numb: nothing would shock her. All she felt as she put one hand in the bag and sifted through the mess of papers was a sense of wonder, of unreality. Idly, she picked up one of the papers and looked at it. It was an invoice: unpaid. The next one was a lengthy, itemized bill: also unpaid. The rest were the same: either unpaid or unopened. She let them sink back into the bag and looked up at Dennis. 'Why didn't you tell me?' There was no reproach in her voice, no hurt and no anger. It was just a question.

'What was the point?' Dennis almost shouted. Agitated, he looked around the room, searching for the whisky decanter. 'You'd never find out cos I was going to make everything all right.' It was a child's response, spoken in a high, childlike voice, pathetically defiant.

Su-Lin got to her feet. 'I don't understand,' she said. 'We've . . . we've just had a holiday; you bought me two new dresses. Where did that money come from?'

Dennis smiled suddenly. The smile was directed not at her face but at her stomach. 'You deserved it.'

Su-Lin felt sick – and slightly scared. Bills stuffed in suitcases; sudden holidays in Malacca; expensive new dresses; banks chasing them. Peter Yang making offers. None of it made sense. And nor did Dennis. She looked up at him and saw a new brightness in his eyes. An unnerving brightness.

'I'm not going to stop trying,' he said, 'just because I've told you.'

She couldn't leave him now, she thought. She *couldn't*. She would do the other thing – but she wouldn't leave him. The decision helped her snap out of her listlessness. Suddenly businesslike, she galvanized herself into positive action.

'Right,' she said. 'We give notice on our lease tomorrow. I'll talk to the bank . . .' Suddenly she stopped, beset by a new worry. 'Do we owe money to the lawyers?'

Dennis's expression was all the answer she needed.

'Okay,' she sighed. 'We can rent somewhere in Mongkok till we know things are going to work out.'

Dennis was appalled. 'Oh yeah?' he sneered. 'And what am I going to do in Mongkok?' He spat out the last word. For him it carried connotations of heat, sweat, the fetid bird-market, street-stalls – and worst of all, poverty. 'I'm an English businessman, for Christ's sake! Nobody's going to buy fruit and bloody veg from me, are they?' He gestured wildly, maniacally round the room. 'This is what I do; this is *me*!' Then his anger evaporated and the strange, eerily bright smile returned. 'We can't bring up our child in Mongkok,' he all but cooed.

But Su-Lin had turned on her heel and into the bed-room. All the lights were on, leaving Dennis, when he followed her, in no doubt as to what she was doing. She was rummaging under the bed for their suitcases.

'Look,' he pleaded as she extracted one, threw it open and then went over to the wardrobe. 'Look at me, Su-Lin. You know I can do it. Two contracts,' he said with a sudden, easy smile. 'That's all I need.'

Su-Lin did as she was bid and looked at him.

'One,' he corrected as he clocked her expression. 'One decent contract and I swear to God all this will go away.'

Slowly, Su-Lin stepped away from the case and drew herself up to her full height, her full five feet. Wouldn't he ever learn, she asked herself? Hadn't he ever consid-ered that the burden he put on her was becoming intolerable? She was sick to death of his violent mood swings, of his secrecy, his sly smiles, his shouting and his pleading. He was a fully grown man. It was about time he started acting like one. It was the last consideration that made her blurt out her confession.

'I can't have this baby, Dennis! We can't have this baby!'

Dennis didn't hear her. Not properly. What had she said?

'What', he asked, looking guarded, 'are you talking about?'

It was done now. No turning back. 'I've been to see Dr Sunny. I've . . . made another appointment.'

'Dr Sunny?'

'The obstetrician.' Su-Lin left the suitcase and walked over to Dennis. She smiled, sadly but confidently, and took his face in her hands. 'It's not just this, the business . . . I didn't know, anyway. It's just that I'm not ready.'

Dennis's eyes, unfocused but bluer, brighter than ever, were inches from her own.

'Neither', she whispered, 'are you.'

Dennis shook his head. 'Su-Lin. Please don't do this to me. You can't say this.'

Su-Lin dropped her hands. 'I'm not', she said with infinite sadness, 'going to watch you kill yourself. Not for me or anyone else! Do you understand, Dennis? *Do* you? I watch you doing all that work and . . . and *fighting* with everything you've got, fighting with everyone around, and it makes me feel useless. You don't seem to need me. I . . . I love you,' she continued, averting her eyes, 'but I don't seem to make any difference, Dennis. I don't want to go through all that again – and especially not with a baby . . . We can start again when the timing's right . . . Dennis?' The last word was spoken in sudden fear, not anger. 'Dennis, what're you doing? *Dennis!* What are you *doing?*'

Dennis was pushing her back onto the bed. Su-Lin's body knew it, but her brain didn't want to acknowledge the fact. The *way* he was pushing her was wrong. Then, as she gasped for breath, he was on top of her, smothering her with kisses. There was a strange wetness about his face. Dennis was crying. With a monumental effort, she pushed him off. 'Dennis! I can't breathe!'

'I'm sorry,' he said as he watched her take great gulps of air. Then, suddenly, he glared at her. 'What about your lot? Your family?' he sneered. 'Don't they get the casting vote? They usually do.'

'They don't even know I'm pregnant,' gasped Su-Lin.

Then Dennis grabbed her wrists. His eyes, while staring, were completely unfocused. Whatever they saw was not in that bedroom, was not real. But Su-Lin was looking at something all too terrifyingly real. She was staring at madness.

'Dennis,' she gasped, trying to raise herself from under his bulk.

'I'm sorry,' he repeated. Then he shoved a handkerchief into her mouth and proceeded to bind her wrists tightly together.

Fitz couldn't understand why or where it had all gone wrong. One minute he had been playing cards and the next he was involved – as were seemingly all the occupants of the bar – in a full-scale fight. Tables had been overturned; people were standing up and screaming at each other; heavily made-up girls were shrieking and diving for cover, and Freddie Cheung was heading briskly towards the door. Fitz had no idea how many whiskies he had consumed since he had started drinking at the university bar – but it hadn't been enough to make him hallucinate. What was happening in front of his eyes – right in front of his eyes – was definitely not a figment of his imagination: his opponent at cards was threatening him with what had to be a machete. As he also had Fitz pinned against the bar and was screaming at him in Cantonese, there wasn't much doubt about who had the upper hand.

'For Christ's sake!' jabbered Fitz. 'You won! You won, for God's sake! What the hell's going on?'

The wailing of sirens and the sudden arrival of several uniformed policemen told Fitz exactly what was going on: the fight had been reported. That it had been reported as a 'major racial disturbance' was something Fitz would not find out until later. His would-be murderer, seeing the policemen burst in, was bent on not being around to find out anything at all: he made a run for the back exit. But one of the policemen was too quick for him; he brandished his gun in a manner that brooked no argument. Fitz's assailant came to an abrupt halt.

Through his haze of alcohol, Fitz was dimly aware of someone being ushered towards him by Freddie. He sobered up almost immediately when he saw who it was: Janet Lee Cheung, Freddie's sister. But now, surrounded by men in uniform, herself dressed in a demure grey suit, she carried with her an unmistakable air of authority; she carried her title of Detective Chief Inspector in her aura rather than on her sleeve. Before Fitz could articulate the wisecrack that was slowly forming in his befuddled mind, she grabbed him by the arm and steered him up the staircase. Tight-lipped and still without having said a word, she marched him to the car parked outside and practically threw him inside.

Unwisely, Fitz tried to resist. 'I think it's brilliant, you know,' he yelled at Janet in particular and the world in general. 'The rest of the world at least tries to fake democracy, to pretend it's civilized. But in Hong Kong, that's bollocks.' He waved his arms around, illustrating his disgust. 'Here it's "show us your money and you've got a life!" I love it! You live or die by your wedge.' Behind him, Freddie tried to help his sister ease him into the vehicle.

Fitz was having none of it. 'If life were that simple everywhere, I wouldn't be such a misfit! Did you see,' he added in tones of almost childish incredulity, 'the *size* of that bloody thing?!'

Freddie rolled his eyes. 'Just say thank you,' he said through pursed lips.

Suddenly Fitz turned to Janet and grinned. 'What's Cantonese for "thank you"?'

Janet glared at him. 'Get in the car,' she barked in her precise, American-accented English.

Fitz got in. In the silence that followed his outburst, several unsavoury thoughts penetrated his brain. One was that he had started the fight in the bar. Another was that Freddie, by calling his sister, had saved his hide: any other member of the police force would have had him in handcuffs. The last thought was that he had made an enemy of Janet Lee Cheung. Thank God, he mused, that they would never have to work together.

Janet Lee Cheung, straight-backed and po-faced in the passenger seat of the car, was thinking exactly the same thing. The sooner Fitz left Hong Kong the better. She hated his arrogance, his alarmingly manic energy and the edge of danger he seemed to carry with him. People like that, she reflected as the car entered the tunnel to take them back to the mainland, were not welcome here.

Someone like that, however, was driving through the tunnel at the same time. He was going in the opposite direction; to Kowloon and one of the container ports on the peninsula. There, in a shipping crate that bore his own name, he was going to deposit the most precious cargo he had ever handled.

In the boot of the car, a terrified Su-Lin Tang struggled in vain to free herself from the knots that bound her, the gag that silenced her and the blindfold that confirmed she was heading towards oblivion.

Chapter Two

Janet Lee Cheung's day began as badly as the previous one had ended. Had Freddie not been her brother and had Gordon Ellison not been her boss, she would have had no compunction about arresting Fitz. As it was, she had escorted him back to the hotel he was staying in, had waited for Freddie to escort him to his room, and had then departed with her brother. The only solace she derived from the whole episode was that Fitz was staying in a seedy backpackers' hotel near the YMCA.

'Why on earth', she had asked Freddie, 'is he staying in that flea-pit?'

'Because', came the simple and slightly sheepish answer, 'the university's paying.'

Janet had laughed like a drain.

*

She wasn't laughing in the morning. At eight-thirty, she received a phone call telling her that Peter Yang had been murdered.

Inured to the concept of death by dint of her profession, Janet was nevertheless stunned. Peter Yang was a big shot in Hong Kong. His name was always in the financial pages; that of his wife in the social pages. The Yangs were wealthy, high-profile and, so it was rumoured, totally above-board. But the murder of a prominent businessman in Hong Kong usually meant only one thing – a Triad killing. Peter Yang, in his business dealings, must have crossed swords with the world of organized crime.

Yet the main reason for Janet's stunned reaction to Yang's death was the fact that it could present her with the biggest break of her career. Saddened as she was that someone had been murdered, she was realistic enough to know that, because of the identity of that particular someone, the investigation would gain almost as high a profile as the deceased himself had enjoyed. Ellison, she knew, would let her handle the case: he was too jaded, too uninterested, too near to going back to England to bother with Peter Yang. And Janet was far too ambitious to let this one pass.

The eight-thirty call came from the station. Yang, it transpired, had been killed in his office – presumably the previous evening. The cleaner, the duty officer told her, had found his body. The patrol policemen were there now. The forensic people were on their way. Would Janet go there immediately to take charge of the proceedings?

Janet would. It took her a mere fifteen minutes, siren blaring, to get from her apartment in Mid-Levels to Central Building, headquarters of Yang Associates.

Chaos reigned outside the building. Why not, thought Janet furiously, have a full-blown drama as well as a crisis? Whoever had assumed control of the situation was not making a good job of it. Yang's business occupied only one floor of the enormous building, yet it seemed that the occupants of every other floor were milling about and jabbering excitedly at each other, gesticulating wildly and adding to the mayhem caused by the flashing lights and wailing sirens. Janet suspected – rightly, as she later found out – that one of the policemen had told a member of the public that Peter Yang had been found murdered in his office. All Hong Kong would know about it before the morning was out. Not good news, thought Janet as she barked orders at the officers outside. She hadn't even seen the corpse; she didn't know how Yang had been murdered – or why. There was a time and a place for releasing information to the public. Now was not that time.

The offices of Yang Associates, as indicated by the legend on the nameplate in the marble foyer, were on the second floor of the building. Easy enough, thought Janet as she eschewed the lift in favour of the stairs, for someone to break in – even from the outside. The adjacent hotchpotch of buildings had balconies and mezzanines at strange levels; air-conditioning units all over the place; walkways and escalators and glass walls that made it difficult to establish whether or not you were under or above ground, let alone what floor you were on.

The forensic officers had got there before her. Peter Yang's inner office, an oasis of understated expense, was a hive of – organized – activity. Benny Ho, Janet's junior detective, was also there, calmly surveying the scene and noting down the layout of the room. A police medic was examining the body. Janet grimaced as she joined him behind the desk: the late Peter Yang was not a pretty sight.

'There's a sign', said Benny Ho, 'of a break-in over there.'

Janet followed his glance, frowned, and went over to the internal window. Sure enough, one of the large panes *was* broken – yet all the glass was outside, not inside Yang's office. Janet smiled a grim, humourless smile. Whoever had killed Yang hadn't had to break in; whoever it was had smashed the glass purely to make it look like an outside job. Peter Yang, then, had been expecting his killer. Had known the man, the woman, or indeed the people who had hated him enough to want to end his life.

Janet looked at her watch. The few reporters she had seen outside would, by now, have been joined by more of their number. TV crews would be arriving any moment. She had to get to headquarters. Had to talk to Ellison, to issue a statement; to orchestrate, if nothing else, a damage-limitation exercise.

Instructing Benny Ho to take charge of the crime scene, leaving the forensic people to their careful and minute dusting of every inch of the office, she left the building.

54

Outside, the pandemonium was, if anything, worse. Tens of reporters swarmed towards her like locusts as she emerged. Thrusting microphones in her face, they bombarded her with questions.

'Detective Chief Inspector: can you confirm that Peter Yang has been murdered?'

'Is it true he was decapitated?'

'Can you confirm that the killing bears the hallmark of the 14K Triad?'

'Was it suicide?'

Janet ignored them all. Slowly yet purposefully, protected by two officers, she made her way through the throng towards a waiting unit car. She managed to remain cool and unflustered until she was in the back seat of the vehicle. Then she leaned back and closed her eyes. This, she thought, was going to be a nightmare. The press, the public and one of the most powerful families in Hong Kong were all going to be baying for blood. And until they got the killer's blood, Janet's would do.

An hour later, it was clear that trying to limit the damage would be a futile exercise. Despite the fact that police headquarters had neither confirmed nor denied that the dead man was Peter Yang, the news was out – and everyone believed it.

Gordon Ellison was particularly displeased. He had been hoping that his last few months in Hong Kong would pass quietly and that he would be thrown bouquets when he left. Now it looked like brickbats would be hurled instead.

'We need', he said to Janet as he hurried down the corridor outside his office, 'to get outside help.'

Janet begged to differ. 'I don't need outside help!' she replied with outraged vehemence. 'It's a business killing.'

Ellison rounded on her. 'It bloody isn't! Peter Yang's a personal friend. And your "business killing"', he snapped as he pushed open the door at the end of the corridor, 'implies that he got his hands dirty. I keep track of all my personal friends.'

Arrogant, patronizing bastard, thought Janet. She wanted to hit him. Instead, with admirable restraint, she pointed out that, as Peter was so wealthy, it was not unlikely that he had crossed *someone* along the way.

'If we have to go *looking*,' replied her boss, 'it won't be significant, will it?' Then he fumbled in his pocket and extracted a packet of cigarettes. 'Oh,' he added with a vague smile, 'close the door, would you?'

Exasperated, Janet slammed the door behind her. They were in a utility-cum-store room. Vacuums and buffer machines were ranked against the walls. At the far end, two uniformed cleaners were doing what Ellison had entered the room to do: they were having a sly fag. Seeing Ellison, they both smiled sheepishly. Ellison barely noticed them. They shrugged at each other and carried on smoking.

'I've got reporters', moaned Ellison as he lit his cigarette and inhaled more deeply than Janet thought possible, 'telling me what I had for dinner the last time I was seen in a restaurant with Peter. I've got two of the most expensive lawyers in Hong Kong – the widow's lawyers – squatting in my office asking for my "plan of action". Christ, Janet,' he added as he took another desperate drag, 'the body was only found two hours ago!'

Janet was getting increasingly irritated. Ellison's plaintive cries of woe were bad enough; the fact that he was hiding in a broom-cupboard having a clandestine cigarette made the situation even more bizarre.

But Ellison hadn't finished. 'And', he said after another furious exhalation, 'I've got a meeting in five minutes with his royal highness the sodding Commissioner.'

Bully for you, thought Janet. She remained silent, yet something in her expression registered with Ellison: even he realized his histrionics were a little over the top.

'Look,' he said with a sudden smile. 'This isn't good news for either of us. I go in May. You walk neatly into the job, yes? But not if this one falls through. You don't', he added with a piercing look and what Janet recognized was the hint of a threat, 'want to be posted to some refugee crowd-control unit, do you?'

Janet nearly hit him.

'All that's required', he finished calmly, 'is throwing everything we've got at it.'

They both knew exactly what he meant.

'We don't', said Janet, knowing the protest was hopeless, 'need *him*.'

Ellison tried to soften the blow. 'He's something to throw at the press.'

'But why don't we just investigate the case and throw *that* at the press?'

'Janet, *please!*' Ellison stubbed out his cigarette. The look on his face told Janet her objections went with it. 'We've got Edward Fitzgerald in Hong Kong,' he said. 'He's one of the best criminal psychologists there is – so we use him.'

Janet stared long and hard at her boss. Then she nodded and left the room, slamming the door as she did so.

Ellison breathed a sigh of relief. Then, as he made to follow Janet, the doubt set in. Edward Fitzgerald and Janet Lee Cheung? Did he want to solve a murder – or cause another one?

Fitz had a hangover. The hotel proprietor's children had woken him up by screaming and shouting in the corridor outside his room. The proprietor himself made sure he didn't get back to sleep by marching into the room half an hour later and demanding payment for the week that Fitz had been a 'guest'. Fitz offered to write a behaviour modification programme for his children instead. The proprietor didn't understand. Even if he had, he wouldn't have found it funny. He wanted cash. Every week – and this fat *gweilo* knew that.

The fat *gweilo* promised to go out and cash some travellers cheques as soon as he was dressed. As he shaved in the flyblown mirror, he rued the day he had decided to sacrifice part of his hotel allowance in favour of more spending money. And he also rued the day – the same one, he remembered – that he had met Freddie Cheung. Last night had been all his fault. And, he thought savagely, there had surely been no need to involve that

58

po-faced stuck-up sister of his. As he dressed, he brought his mind back to the earlier, sober meeting he had had with Freddie's sister. She had been dismissive of his lecture. Arrogant. Superior. Fitz had seen the signs many times. The woman was obviously insecure.

The woman was also in his room when he returned from his cheque-cashing mission. If she had intended to catch him on the hop, then she succeeded. Fitz hadn't understood that the proprietor's Cantonese rantings down in the lobby had not, on this occasion, been about money but about the fact there was a policewoman in his bedroom. He didn't like the police. They tended to ask too many questions: questions to which Mr Wang generally didn't have appropriate answers.

Fitz, however, was too smart an operator, too seasoned a player of games of the upper hand to show anything but polite curiosity. He managed to swallow his surprise almost as soon as he saw Janet, looking somehow triumphant as well as enigmatic, standing at the foot of his bed.

'I don't recall', he said with a grin, 'ordering anything from "the other menu".'

Janet pursed her lips. Was he, as she suspected, likening her unto a prostitute. She decided to ignore the insult. 'I've just had you removed', she said, 'from the university.'

This time Fitz was visibly shocked. He compensated, swiftly, by sneering. 'Democracy in action?' he scoffed. 'On what grounds have you "had me removed"?'

'One,' said Janet as if she were ticking items off a list, 'I think your lectures are under-researched, over-personalized bullshit. Two, Commander Ellison wants your professional advice.' She spoke the last two words with a delicate smile of distaste.

'Tough titty. I'm not for hire. This is a lecture tour,' said Fitz in his most patronizing voice, 'not the lucky dip.'

But Janet knew all about the gambling. Well primed by Freddie, she also knew that Fitz – not to mention his estranged wife – was in dire need of funds.

'He'll pay good money,' she said. Then, adopting Fitz's sneer, she added that good money was better news for his wife than it was for him 'if your gambling's anything to go by'.

Fitz glared at her. The bloody woman, he thought, had gone for the jugular, tweaked the Achilles' heel.

'Tell Commander Ellison', he said without batting an eyelid, 'that I'm flattered.'

'Tell him yourself.' Janet stalked past him and into the landing. 'Let's go.'

She did not see the look Fitz bestowed on her departing back.

The words 'under-researched and over-personalized bullshit' were still ringing in Fitz's ears during the short journey to Central Building. They provided another clue to Janet Lee Cheung's personality. Why, wondered Fitz, did she feel so threatened by him? Her professional pride was obviously piqued by Ellison's decision to take him on board – but there was more to it than that. She was frightened of Fitz. Frightened, perhaps, by the concept of psychology? She wouldn't be the first law enforcer he had encountered who thought that criminal psychologists were out to score points over the police rather than to help them.

Unaware of his analysis, Janet told him about Peter Yang's death. Fitz studied her face as she did so: he was more interested in what she *wasn't* telling rather than the facts she was trotting out. A prominent and hugely wealthy businessman; an important member of Hong Kong society; obviously, Janet said, a business killing. But, said Fitz to himself, Ellison's not at all sure about that, is he? And you have your doubts as well.

'Business killing?' he said. 'That's a euphemism for little fingers, right? He held up his own, not so little, fingers. 'The old pinkie-ectomy?'

'Triads don't do fingers. That's Yakuza. Japanese.'

Fitz refused to be riled by her cool dismissiveness. 'I'm very keen on my little finger,' he said conversationally. 'In Britain, it's an essential tool – more important than a penis in some regions. And it's not the size, it's what you do with it.' Only a slight tightening of Janet's knuckles on the steering-wheel betrayed her irritation. 'In Edinburgh,' continued Fitz, 'we use it for ordering cakes while we're drinking tea. In Manchester you use it for picking scabs off your impetigo.' His accurate, if unusual social commentary on the extremes of the two cities failed to impress Janet. Worse, her expression indicated that, where Hong Kong was concerned, Fitz was a complete beginner: pinkie or no pinkie. This was her patch. 'So you see,' finished an undaunted Fitz, 'it's quite versatile. I'd hate to lose one of mine.'

Janet seemed to cheer up at that possibility. Smiling, she pulled out of the traffic, turned into Prater Street, and parked on a double yellow line outside a large smoked-glass building.

'Here we are,' she said. 'Central Building.'

'Hmm.' Not, thought Fitz, one of the architectural wonders of Hong Kong. Plain and businesslike. He got out of the car and, with Janet leading the way, entered the building. Had the killer done a plain and business-like job on Peter Yang? Janet had, for reasons of her own, said nothing about how he was killed.

Gordon Ellison was already there. So, palpably excited, was the police pathologist. Never before had he had the chance to examine such a famous corpse. The implications, career-wise, could be enormous. Desperate to get down on his hands and knees and begin work, he was being thwarted by Ellison. The policeman was insisting that the 'famous criminal psychologist' had to see the body as it had been found.

'Commander Ellison,' said Janet to Fitz as they walked into the room. 'You've met.'

Fitz knew that.

Ellison stepped forward to shake hands. 'Thanks for your co-operation, Doctor.' He gestured vaguely to the body behind the desk. 'It's a bugger, this one, because he's so well known.'

Fitz nodded and walked round the desk. Yang was

lying, awkwardly as only the dead can do, half on his back and half on his side. The upper half of his torso, including his head, was covered with what looked like his own jacket. So, thought Fitz, even the forensics people had been offended by whatever had killed him.

Fitz leaned down and pulled at the jacket. It fell away to reveal an unblemished torso – and a head that was no longer round. One side of it had been hit so hard that it had caved in; collapsing into itself in a mass of congealed blood, broken bone and foul-smelling matter and tissue that had once been the brain behind Yang Associates. Fitz's only reaction was an almost imperceptible twitch of the nostrils. Apart from the fact that he had seen far worse sights, he was well aware that Janet Lee Cheung and Commander Ellison were watching him intently; gauging his reaction; judging his competence.

'I'm genuinely convinced', said Ellison in a drinks-party sort of voice, 'that it's not a contract killing.'

Fitz straightened up and turned to face him. 'Who's arguing?' he said.

Ellison looked accusingly at Janet. Janet, defiant, looked at Fitz. Then she walked towards the body and pointed to the hands, half-hidden under the desk.

'Look,' she said.

Fitz looked. The hands had been intricately bound together, fingers straight, to form a pyramid. Or a steeple.

'Somebody', said Janet, 'is sending messages.'

'A prayer', intoned Fitz, 'for the dying.' Then he looked back at Ellison. 'That's not a Triad calling-card?'

63

'No.'

'There's Triad business,' said Janet, 'and there's business.'

She turned to the increasingly impatient pathologist. 'Okay. He's all yours.'

For a moment, there was silence while the pathologist, crouching on hands and knees, got closer to Peter Yang than he had ever dreamed possible. Later, in the calmer atmosphere of the mortuary, he would be able to make a detailed examination, to establish to the best of his ability the cause and time of death. Now, all he would be able to do was to give these policemen something to go on.

Fitz prowled the room while the pathologist examined the body, talking into his tape recorder as he did so. He appeared to relish what he was doing, to be detailing his finds with the enthusiasm of an archaeologist at a successful dig. Fitz was more interested in the other objects in the room; particularly in a large silver trophy lying on the floor. It bore faint traces of forensic dust – and not-so-faint ones of blood. Nodding to himself, Fitz then looked around again, searching for the normal resting-place of the trophy. He found it on a high shelf behind the desk in the shape of a plinth bearing a small silver plaque. He stepped closer and peered upwards. The plaque boasted the legend 'The Royal Hong Kong Jockey Club' and, underneath, Peter Yang's name alongside that of a horse. Turning round, eyebrows raised in inquisition, Fitz looked at the pathologist. The man was also looking at the plinth – and jabbering away in

Cantonese. Janet opened her mouth to interpret for Fitz's benefit. Fitz, however, beat her to it.

'He'll sign off the time of death', he said in slightly weary tones, 'to within three hours. He couldn't say precisely whether it was amateur, professional or multiple.' Janet and Ellison gaped, open-mouthed, as he continued. 'And he won't commit himself to a murder weapon till the autopsy.'

There was a short, stunned silence during which a horrified Janet remembered calling Fitz an arrogant bastard – in Cantonese – in front of him the previous day. 'You . . . er, you speak Cantonese?' she said at last.

'No. I speak post-mortem to intermediate second year.' Fitz's inflection suggested that Janet was somewhere below that level.

'Is there any sign', he said to Ellison, 'of robbery.'

'We don't know yet.' This from a thin-lipped Janet.

Fitz contemplated that in silence for a moment and then turned to the trophy. 'How heavy's that thing?'

This time it was the pathologist, fluent in English and intensely annoyed by Fitz's earlier show of one-upmanship, who snapped back. 'Not heavy enough. Are you', he continued, 'the criminal psychologist?' Are you, the subtext read, the waste of space?

Fitz just grinned. 'Oh. You don't need them here, apparently?'

The pathologist glared at him. 'We're more straight-forward about murder than you are.' Then, as if to prove a no-nonsense attitude, he walked over to the trophy, bagged it, and deposited it in his large medical bag. 'I'll do the autopsy', he said to Ellison as he walked out of the room, 'at about five.'

Seemingly unaware of the nascent hatred all around him, Ellison looked at Fitz. 'The press', he said with a frown, 'have found out you're on board.'

Now how long have I been on board, thought Fitz? How could they possibly have had time to find out? And from whom?

Ellison suddenly avoided Fitz's eye. 'You may', he continued, 'be squeezed for speculation, but I'd rather you just talked about your qualifications, your experience in Urban Homicide in Birmingham.'

Or perhaps I could tell them about what I did in my holidays, thought Fitz.

'Manchester,' he corrected. 'And it's not a hobby, Gordon.' He scratched his chin and made a show of twirling on his size tens.

'What're you offering?' he asked suddenly.

Both Janet and Ellison looked at him with barely concealed dislike.

'Two thousand a day plus expenses,' said the latter.

'Sterling?'

'Hong Kong dollars.'

'Hmm.' Two hundred quid, near as dammit. Fitz wondered if they knew what the university had been giving him. Probably. 'Accommodation?' he ventured.

'No,' said Janet at the same time as Ellison said 'yes'.

'*New* accommodation?' pressed Fitz.

'Where?' said a suspicious Ellison, beset by visions of a suite at the Peninsula.

'Ritz Carlton.'

Janet looked thunderstruck. She knew perfectly well that the university had been paying him a thousand a day, flea-pit included. 'He's got debts', she said to Ellison, 'at the Tsang Te Hotel, which is pretty hard to achieve.'

Ellison had never been to the Tsang Te. He rather felt he didn't want to. 'Oh all right,' he said with a sigh. 'Ritz Carlton it is.' At least, he thought, we can keep an eye on him there.

But Fitz hadn't finished. 'I'm not used to working alone,' he said with mild petulance.

'You won't work alone. You'll report directly to DCI Cheung' – he indicated the smirking Janet – 'who'll report to me. This', he added, 'is one of the best-staffed police forces in the world. We have all the resources you need.'

Fitz wasn't so sure. Resources, in this place, meant money. 'Not', he said, 'if the only motive you're used to is money. There's a detective in England', he added as if the thought had only just occurred to him, 'I have a special relationship with.'

Janet's eyes narrowed. She could bet she knew the nature of the 'special relationship'.

Ellison was now beginning to regret his decision to take Fitz on board. Yet the fact remained that he had just embarked on the highest-profile, most-publicity-generating investigation of his career. A lot hinged on this – and even Ellison realized that the reputation of the entire Royal Hong Kong Police was at stake. The world – certainly the business world – would monitor this investigation very carefully. It wouldn't do, in six months' time, for the unsolved murder of Peter Yang to be Britain's last legacy to Hong Kong.

'Well,' he said with obvious reluctance, 'I'll have to liaise with the Home Office.' He took a pad and pen out of his breast pocket. 'What's his name?'

'Jane Penhaligon,' said Fitz. 'Greater Manchester Police. I'll want her on the case with me.' Detective Sergeant Jane Penhaligon. Panhandle, he called her. His partner in solving crime. His partner, afterwards, in much more than that. And latterly – what? Fitz didn't know. He didn't know what their relationship was now: he didn't even know if they *had* a relationship.

Nor did he know that Janet Lee Cheung was fixing him with a penetrating – and knowing – look. So often accused, like the rest of her race, of being inscrutable, she was a past master at reading the supposedly blank expression that Fitz was wearing.

Ellison's mind, however, was still on his budget. 'Are you absolutely confident', he asked Fitz, 'that you can be of assistance?'

Fitz nodded. 'This murder', he said with absolute confidence, 'is not about money.'

Arrogant bastard, thought Janet. 'We don't know that yet,' she said.

'Was his wallet intact?'

Damn the man, thought Janet, remaining silent. How does he know?

Fitz nodded, correctly taking her silence for assent.

'Okay,' he said, suddenly animated. 'Forget the victim.

68

Picture your killer. He's here on a different mission. Completely unarmed. When something goes wrong and the shit hits the fan,' he said with a gesture towards Yang's desk, 'does he shoot him? No. Knife him? No. He stoves his head in with a nickel-plated trophy.' Fitz waved an arm again, his gesture encompassing the marble elephant on a side table; the huge blue and white vase in the corner; the heavy jade artefacts in the wall-cabinet. 'There's half a dozen heavier objects in that office, but which does he go for? That one.' He pointed at the plinth high on the shelf. 'A trophy on a shelf so high, he has to reach for it. That', he said to his now transfixed listeners, 'is your murder weapon. The man *knew* his victim. He *envied* his victim. He resented the power of a man with a member's trophy from the Royal Hong Kong Jockey Club – one of the richest institutions in the world, yes?' The last statement was half guess-work, prompted by some dim memory. The nods of agreement from Ellison and Janet told him it was true. 'So,' he continued, 'it's not straightforward murder, it's *disorganized communication.* If you're checking his contacts, keep your eyes peeled for the *under*achievers.'

Ellison's eyes had nearly popped out of his head. 'I say, Dr Fitzgerald, that's absolutely bloody *fascinating.*' Beaming broadly, feeling totally vindicated for his decision to bring Fitz in, he turned triumphantly to Janet. 'You see?'

But Janet was going to need more convincing. Talk was all very well, she thought, but it didn't necessarily get results.

Fitz ignored her and returned Ellison's smile. 'You won't get any of that from an autopsy. And please: I feel like I know you. Call me Fitz.'

Dennis was full of energy. He had, he felt, achieved a lot over the past twenty-four hours. Partly because of that, he was also full of renewed resolution; new ideas. He knew exactly what had to be done.

Last night, he hadn't been so sure. Returning from Kowloon, he had found himself unsure of what to do next; unsure, even, about what he had just done. And then he had remembered why he had done it. Punishment. And, of course, protection. It was vital to keep people protected from unwelcome things: his mother had taught him that. Or rather, she had shown him that. That was where the dark came in. Darkness. How different things looked in the light. It was then, as he drove out of the tunnel from the muted light to the blazing neon of the island, that the thought had occurred to him. There was someone else who had let him down. Someone else who needed to be taught a lesson; to be punished.

Peter Yang had been more than a little surprised to see him. It had been, after all, well after nine o'clock. Peter had been preparing to go home; had made enough money for the day. Yet he had pretended to be pleased to see Dennis. He had, when Dennis had walked in unannounced, even professed to be delighted, to be glad that Dennis had changed his mind about selling the business.

It hadn't occurred to Dennis to change his mind.

Now, driving across the island in the bright light of the morning, he recalled how he had acted. My, how he had acted.

'I can make the cheque out', Peter had said, 'to whoever you want.'

'I want it made out to the business.'

Peter hadn't liked that one. Even though he was signing money over to someone else, it irked him that the money would go to waste. 'You'll wipe it out in taxes,' he had said.

But Dennis had been adamant.

Then he had surprised Peter, shocked him by producing the faxes that he had gone back to the office to retrieve before going to Central Building. He recalled all of them: he had fumed over them, worked himself up into a lather when none of them had received a reply. 'Peter, give me a ring when you've got a minute.' 'Peter, you're obviously up to your eyeballs but give me a ring when you've time for a drink.' Still no reply. 'Peter, communicate!!!' Jocular, that one. But still silence. Dennis knew that Peter had seen the faxes, that he had assumed Dennis was after a favour. And so he had ignored them.

In a way, Dennis supposed he *had* been asking a favour. He had wanted to ask Peter to be the baby's godfather.

Peter had been mortified when Dennis had told him, rigid with shock. But by then it was too late for excuses. Dennis had worked himself up into a lather all over again and this time he hadn't been able to help himself.

He would do better today, he swore. He was calmer, more collected, much more sure of what he was going to

71

do and how he was going to do it. Perhaps, because he had no personal knowledge of the man, he wouldn't get so upset. And maybe, after the nice drive to Repulse Bay, he would be in a better mood. On the other hand, maybe not. Dennis's hands tightened on the steering-wheel. Dr Sunny was, after all, nothing but a butcher.

Dennis hadn't known that when he had first heard the name. Sunny, he was told, was one of the best. Rich, idle ladies who lunched – *Tai Tais*, in local parlance – swore by him for their various and generally illusory illnesses. That was why Dennis had insisted Su-Lin register with him. It was as important, Dennis knew, to have the right doctor as it was to have the right dressmaker, manicurist, personal dry-cleaner, tennis coach and even plant man. Su-Lin, who had previously been perfectly happy with her family doctor in Shau Kei Wan, had laughed about Dennis's latest 'find' but had nevertheless acquiesced. Dr Sunny, she knew, was a specialist in 'women's problems', and it would do no harm to have an expert to make sure that everything stayed in working order. And one day, of course, she would be pregnant. Dr Sunny would make sure all went well. Su-Lin hadn't told Dennis that Dr Sunny would also make sure – no questions asked – that an abortion could go equally well. Discreet, safe and utterly reliable, he was the rich person's answer to Mongkok's back-street butchers.

But now Dennis knew that. Silly Dr Sunny, he thought. And silly Su-Lin. Dennis smiled to himself as he emerged from the Aberdeen tunnel on his way south.

The sensation of being underground reminded him of last night's journey through the Eastern tunnel; the journey to Kowloon with his precious cargo in the boot. It all seemed such a long time ago. He had achieved so much, even since then. And now he would achieve even more.

Dr Sunny's consulting-rooms faced the sea. Tranquil and calm, they had exactly the right ambience to soothe nervous or scared patients – and many of his patients were both. Dennis, however, was very much in control. Normally the slow journey southwards irritated him; he was usually frustrated by the parking problem in Repulse Bay – and he often found it difficult to find new addresses. Not this time. A mere half-hour after leaving Happy Valley he had reached his destination, found a parking space and, with a smile of satisfaction, was ringing the bell beside the discreet gold nameplate that boasted Dr Sunny's name and qualifications. A minute later he was being shown into the doctor's inner office.

Sunny, carefully and thoroughly washing his hands after his examination of his previous patient, had his back to Dennis as he entered.

'Take a seat,' he announced in Cantonese. Then, turning round, he smiled an apology. For some reason, he had expected this last, new and – according to his receptionist – urgent patient to be a Chinese lady. Had he known that the appointment he had agreed to squeeze in before his afternoon game of golf was for a perfectly fit-looking Englishman, he probably wouldn't have acquiesced. Still, the man was here now.

With practised ease, Sunny disguised his scrutiny of

the man under a welcoming smile. Yes, he thought, this man is perfectly fit. Thirty-five, perhaps? Thick, dark-blond hair. Healthy looking skin. Only the piercing blue eyes betrayed the fact that something was wrong. They were desperate eyes. Dr Sunny sat down opposite Dennis and prepared himself for a long, convoluted story that would go round in circles and finally terminate in his reassuring this man that, no, he hadn't picked up a 'social disease' from the prostitute he had – uncharacter-istically, of course – picked up on a business trip to Bangkok. Sunny had been through the rigmarole many times before.

'So,' he said. 'What can I do for you, Mr . . .?'

But the man in front of him showed no signs of divulging his name. That, too, was not unusual. Either they remained anonymous or they were 'Mr Smith'.

Then came the first surprise. 'My girlfriend', said Dennis as he leaned forward in his seat, 'came to see you last Friday. Su-Lin Tang?'

'Oh. Well . . . let me just . . .' Frowning, the doctor pulled open the small filing cabinet under his desk and looked for the relevant file. He made a show of rummag-ing even though he found it in seconds. There was something about the abrupt, accusatory way the man had asked the question that bothered him. And he remembered Su-Lin Tang anyway. She had come to arrange for a termination. He had a horrible feeling that this man had come on a 'how dare you kill my child?' mission. Dr Sunny had experience of that sort of appointment as well. They could get nasty. He pulled out

74

Su-Lin's file and placed it on the desk in front of him.

'Is Ms Tang with you?' he asked.

Dennis shook his head. 'She's scared. I think you put her off.'

O-oh. Here we go, thought Sunny. 'Scared of what?' he asked in careful, measured tones.

'The abortion.'

Dr Sunny breathed a sigh of relief; a sigh which he sought to disguise as a gentle remonstration. 'I can't', he said, 'discuss this with you. If she wants to come back, or if you come back together, I'll go over the details, but . . .'

'Go over the details for me.' Dennis's voice, sharp now, carried an unmistakable hint of menace. He leaned down for his briefcase and opened it on his lap. 'How much is this going to cost?'

Sunny's outraged reply was forestalled by a knock on the door.

'Yes?' said Sunny, relieved at the interruption.

The door opened a fraction. 'Er . . . Dr Sunny. I, um . . . I left my handbag here . . . under that chair . . . and . . .' The face, that of Dr Sunny's previous patient, was creased with anxiety. The slim white fingers were pulling at the strands of blond hair escaping from the bun. Dr Sunny jumped to his feet and, smiling, retrieved the handbag. Then he walked with it to the door. Clearly relieved, yet with the nervous, distracted smile that she had worn when she had first appeared in his room, Catherine Wilson snatched the bag, muttered a 'thanks' and then turned on her heels. Sunny smiled after her. In a week's time, he reflected, she would have nothing to worry about. If only she knew of the hundreds of young women he had delivered from a similar plight.

His smile disappeared as soon as he turned back to Dennis Philby. He didn't sit down again; just stood at the side of his desk, hoping the implication was clear. 'The termination', he said, 'costs six thousand, five hundred.'

Dennis looked at him over the open lid of the briefcase. 'Six-five? Cheap at the price.'

'Huh?' Dr Sunny was insulted. He charged an extortionate rate for a termination – as he did for everything else. Then he frowned down at Dennis. What was this man here for? To crow about how rich he was? To intimate that the fees were too low – and the operation therefore too unreliable? Damned cheek.

Dennis stood up. 'Cheap,' he repeated.

'Not everyone on this island', said Dr Sunny with unconcealed distaste, 'is as rich as you are.' Then he reached round to the top drawer of his desk and extracted his car keys. 'Miss Tang', he said as he shut the drawer with an air of finality, 'claimed to be perfectly happy with both the price and the process of the termination. If she's changed her mind, then I repeat that either she, or indeed both of you, should make another appointment with my receptionist. Now, if you'll excuse me . . .'

For a moment, Dennis looked as if he wasn't going to be brushed off that easily. Then, suddenly, he laughed. Dr Sunny all but jumped in alarm: the laugh was wild, manic. This man, he thought, is dangerous. Why, he thought with a stab of panic, isn't Miss Tang here with him? What had she said to him? What had he said to *her*? Not wanting to let the man see the sudden fear in his eyes, he marched over to the door and held it open. To his intense relief, his 'patient' took his cue and, with a last, sly smile, left the office.

Dr Sunny found himself returning to his desk, sitting down and taking several very deep breaths. There was something very wrong with that man, he said to himself. He had seen the signs once before. In a hospital for the criminally insane.

Regaining his composure, he looked towards the telephone. The word 'police' echoed in his head. The man was not safe; he had a pregnant girlfriend; he evinced the classic signs of psychosis. Then hard reality hit Dr Sunny. What was he going to tell the police? That he hadn't liked the look in the eyes of a man who wasn't even one of his patients? That the man accused him of being too cheap? The police, he knew, would just laugh him off. Worse, they might direct their enquiries at *him*; question his suitability to practise medicine. No, there was no way he could do anything about what had just happened. Better to forget about it: to banish it from his mind and concentrate on this afternoon's activities. The thought brought a smile to his face. Golf really was the best recipe for clearing the head. Grinning in anticipation of a pleasurable afternoon ahead, he retrieved his briefcase and left the room.

Dennis waited for Dr Sunny on the landing. Concealing himself in the lobby of the service stairs, he could monitor the activity in the foyer through the small window in the door. After a five-minute wait, Dr Sunny appeared from his suite of rooms and, after a cursory glance around him, pressed the lift 'call' button. Dennis bit his lip. He had no way of knowing if Dr Sunny was going to the ground-floor entrance or to the basement car park. After a moment of agonized indecision, Dennis decided on the latter. Dr Sunny could easily afford one of the prohibitively expensive parking permits for the building. Furthermore, Sunny looked like the sort of man who enjoyed his creature comforts: trailing around in the heat looking for a parking space would not be one of them.

Dennis raced down the stairs and emerged, panting, at basement level. The lift, he reckoned, couldn't have beaten him to it. An unsuspecting Dr Sunny would not arrive for another few moments. Enough time to get his breath back; to formulate a plan. Dennis laughed out loud at the latter concept. He already had a plan: he was full of plans. It was funny, he told himself, how easy it was to accomplish things once you had decided on a course of action. Life was getting simpler by the minute.

But not for Dr Sunny. Stepping out of the lift into the dimly lit car park, he wasn't aware that he was being followed until he was next to his car, a sporty little Toyota MR2. He heard the footsteps at the same time as he flashed his remote to unlock the vehicle. With a sudden stab of fear, and even as he turned, he knew whom he would find behind him.

The man who had coolly departed from his office just

minutes before was now looking distinctly ruffled. He was perspiring heavily, and the strange, wild look had come back into his eyes. Desperate to avoid further confrontation, Sunny lunged for his car door. 'Here is not the place', he said as he wrenched it open, 'to discuss your girlfriend's situation.'

But Dennis was suddenly beside him, leering at him – and blocking his way into the car. 'She hasn't *got* a situation,' he said with a twisted smile. 'And who's asking for a discussion?' The gesture that accompanied the last words was crystal clear: discussion-time, said the knife that he whipped out from under his jacket, was over.

Sunny gave a little moan of terror. He felt a queasy sensation in his stomach; a lurch in his bowels. This was not real; he was hallucinating. He closed his eyes and willed normality to come back.

They both heard the footsteps at the same time. Dr Sunny opened his eyes and saw, not thirty feet away, another man walking through the car park. He was not so quick, however, to open his mouth to scream. And then it was too late: Dennis was on him, grinning insanely, pressing the knife to his throat. The confidence that had evaded him for most of his life was with him now. In one swift, deft movement, he had Sunny down on the ground, head against the wheel of his car. Hope abandoned, the doctor stared, wide-eyed with terror, at his assailant.

'I don't *listen* to people like you,' snarled Dennis. Then he jabbed with the knife. A little whimper escaped

Sunny's constricted throat. A tiny drop of blood slipped onto his pristine white shirt.

Dennis bent even closer. 'How old's my child?' he breathed. 'Four and a half months? I'm seeing something there with a chance to grow.' His hand tightened on the knife and his eyes told Sunny that he had finally lost it. His next words confirmed his madness: they tumbled out, conveying nothing except anger and his rage.

'What're you looking at?' he suddenly demanded. 'It's not one thing or the other, so you just bloody well sort it out.' His free hand, seemingly working independently of the rest of his body, waved around, spinning madly above him. It gave Dr Sunny a ray of hope. The other man in the car park would see. Then the slam of a car door and the sound of an engine turning over extinguished that hope.

Sunny groaned again – further enraging Dennis. 'Nobody stands a chance with people like you. You swan about like God, but just look at the state of you. Ha!' He bent further down until his face, distorted by seething, whispering fury, was only an inch from the doctor's. 'You proud of yourself, Doctor?'

Dr Sunny knew that if he spoke in anything more than a whisper the knife would descend. 'My job,' he croaked, 'is to deliver babies. I don't *just* do terminations.'

'No,' replied Dennis, his voice almost drowned by the sound of the other car roaring towards the exit. 'Well, you're certainly not doing this one.' Then he leaned back to get more leverage, lunged forward again and plunged the knife through the other man's throat. The ease of the knife's passage surprised him; the noise pleased him. There was something very *carnal* about the process. To his surprise, he felt himself becoming aroused as the blade sliced neatly into the muscle and punctured the aorta. Dr Sunny looked as if he, too, was aroused. He gurgled and gasped, he moaned and rolled his eyes and his entire body shuddered, wanting yet at the same time willing itself not to succumb to climax.

He was dead by the time the knife pierced the other side of his neck and punctured the car tyre.

Chapter Three

Su-Lin was in the dark. She had, she supposed, been in the dark for a long time now: longer than the duration of her imprisonment. Why hadn't she guessed that Dennis's 'mood swings' were insidious indications of some greater, permanent catastrophe? How had she failed to detect the signs? Or had part of her seen them but refused to acknowledge them? By spending more and more time with her family, she supposed she had not needed to heed them. But she must have known they were there. Why else would she have arranged an abortion? In the depths of her soul, she had realized that Dennis was not to be trusted around a small, defenceless being; that Dennis wasn't normal. That Dennis couldn't cope.

And now this. Su-Lin groaned and, for the umpteenth time, shifted position in the fruitless endeavour to make herself more comfortable. Each time she moved, the shackles chafed against her wrists and her ankles. And each time she moved she was beset by feelings of desperation, of numb fear – but most of all, of disbelief.

She knew where she was. Dennis had taken her on several previous occasions to his shipping crates in the holding-basin off Kowloon. They were red and emblazoned in white on the sides were the words 'Philby Medical'. Dennis was inordinately proud of them. They were shipped all over the Far East; to Australia; even to England. Or at least they used to be. Now most of them, like this one, stood empty.

Su-Lin had been barely conscious when Dennis had bundled her into the boot of his car the previous evening. She had fainted not with pain but with shock; with the same disbelief she was still experiencing: disbelief that her boyfriend, her companion of five years, had taken leave of his senses and was binding her, gagging her and, she assumed, preparing to dispose of her.

But he hadn't disposed of her. Su-Lin vividly recalled the words he had used as, after the car journey, he had opened the heavy metal door of the crate and dragged her in. He had been in tears, stricken by remorse; muttering in seeming confusion. But his words had given the lie to that confusion. 'You are the most important thing in my life,' he had said with an intensity that had frightened Su-Lin. 'Now you're the *two* most important things in my life.' Then he had stared at her for a moment, burning holes in her eyes. By the time Su-Lin had managed to spit out the gag in her mouth, he had clattered his way across the floor of the crate and banged the door behind him. All that was left was the fading echo of metal against metal – and an all-enveloping darkness.

Complete silence had followed. Hours later, morning noises had roused Su-Lin from the torpor into which she had sunk. Less than a hundred yards away, Hong Kong was coming to life. Yet the sound of the ships, the planes overhead, the drilling of nearby construction workers were all muffled by the impenetrable solidity of Su-Lin's prison. She had shouted until she was hoarse, knowing as she did so that her cries were futile. The cargo holding-basin was at the end of a promontory; there were probably other crates on either side of her, and the only people likely to come anywhere near her were the crane drivers who lifted and lowered the heavy containers. Su-Lin's crate was empty, apart from the holdall that Dennis had dumped beside her. That, initially, had given her hope. Surely the crate would soon be lifted, taken to a ship or a loading bay, and opened, ready to receive a cargo? And then she had remembered who the crate belonged to. There would be no movement; neither Philby Medical nor its crates were going anywhere. Nor was she.

It wasn't until later in the morning that she forced herself to contemplate Dennis's plans for her. *Now you're the two most important things in my life.* Dennis wasn't going to kill her. He was going to keep her here until she delivered the baby. Madness had robbed him of all reason – and all considerations of time. Su-Lin was only three-and-a-half months pregnant.

Darkness had again descended by the time Dennis returned. Only tiny flickers from overhead arc-lights penetrated the total blackness of Su-Lin's prison. Her confinement; wasn't that what they called it? How Su-Lin had laughed when she had thought of that. *Look at me!* she had wanted to shout. *Rest, no exertion, calm and silence: I'm only following doctor's orders!* Then she had buried her head in her hands and cried great heaving sobs as she realized that soon she would be following nothing except Dennis's descent into insanity.

She had exhausted herself by the time Dennis appeared. The noise as he opened the door was appallingly loud; his heavy tread across the metal floor even louder. They weren't footsteps; they were the sinister beats of a gong announcing that madness had returned.

But it was only Dennis's eyes that looked mad as, illuminating them both with the light he was carrying, he bent down and kissed her tenderly. His words were matter-of-fact, businesslike. So too were his actions as he dropped a bag beside her and, after his greeting, began to remove items from it. Su-Lin was relieved that his attention was so occupied: he hadn't appeared to notice the fear in her own eyes and the way she flinched and stiffened as he had kissed her. The incongruity of the situation, the macabre tableau of his own devising, completely passed him by.

'Oranges,' he said as he pulled a string basket out of the holdall. 'Juicer.' He looked with approval at the expensive steel item that followed the oranges. He had thought about buying a plastic one, but had dismissed the notion almost immediately. Only the best would do. He turned to the horrified Su-Lin. 'You need as much vitamin C as you can get your hands on. And', he added with a bright smile, 'apparently you can't overdose, because anything you don't use, your body gets rid of.'

So it's true, thought Su-Lin. *The confinement. He's going to keep me here.* The whites of her eyes shone bright in the semi-darkness. A primeval, feral fear gripped her.

But there was more.

'Speaking of which,' added Dennis with, this time, a smile of pure triumph, 'I've also brought you a bucket. Y'know. A potty.' He looked to Su-Lin for approval. She forced herself to nod. 'And', he continued as he delved once more into the holdall, 'other vitamin pills. No vitamin A, though. That's bad for you, bad for the little 'un. Liver damage, if you read the books.'

He's *pleased* with himself, thought Su-Lin with mounting horror. He's like a little boy with a lucky bag. He's even talking like a little boy. And he wants me to congratulate him for being so good. She shuddered. Half-remembered notions of psychology floated into her mind. Was this what Dennis had been like as a little boy? Was this a confused little person who wanted both to strike out on his own and to crawl back into the womb? And how was she supposed to react? She was, she

87

thought, supposed to be as pleased as he was. He wanted approval. She would give it. Ignoring the bile in her throat, the knot of fear in her stomach, she smiled at the man in front of her.

Dennis didn't notice. He was still unloading his shopping. Bottles of tonic, of water, more fruit – dried, this time – and even a small, battery-operated fan appeared from his bag. He lined them up in a neat row beside Su-Lin and then reached with glee for the last item in the bag. 'Stretchband,' he muttered, stroking the elastic tube. Then he looked at Su-Lin. 'D'you know what a stretchband's for? . . . No? Well, y'see . . . it's cardiovascular. Like this.' Still smiling, Dennis stood up, a salesman pitching to a client, and performed a sequence of exercises with the stretchband. His movements were erratic, exaggerated and jerky. 'Guarantees your circulation's absolutely tops,' he panted as he bent and stretched. 'Under your foot,' he said, demonstrating. 'Round your wrist and s-t-r-e-t-c-h! Tightens all your muscles. See?'

His grotesque parodies of an exercise class were the last straw. The tears began to stream down Su-Lin's face.

'Please,' she whispered. 'I just want to go.'

'Where?' Dennis stopped stretching and looked down at her in surprise.

'Home. Take me home.'

Although still smiling, Dennis shook his head. Didn't she understand? This *was* home now. A nice, quiet, peaceful home. And now he had furnished it with all the creature comforts Su-Lin needed. The smile disappeared.

Why was she not pleased with him?

'Dennis. Look at me, please.'

Dennis looked. Su-Lin saw conflict in his expression; a kaleidoscope of emotions battling against each other. He seemed briefly interested, as if he had only just registered her presence. Then he looked upset, hurt to be thwarted in his kind purpose. Then his eyes flickered, his shoulders slumped and he looked pained, defeated and lost.

Careful, thought Su-Lin. Seize the moment, but gently. 'You need', she suggested without a trace of accusation, 'to see a doctor.'

It was the wrong thing to say. 'S'all right,' said Dennis. 'I've found one.' Suddenly he was no longer lost. The manic grin was back – and with it came the anger. He knelt beside Su-Lin again and pressed his bloated, unshaven face close to hers; so close that she could smell his stale breath. His clothes, too, smelled unclean.

'You'd have gone to your sister's apartment,' he accused her, 'and ignored the phone for a couple of days, wouldn't you? Dr Sunny could've done the business and I'd have been none the wiser. Three-day lovers' tiff, eh?' He leaned back, arching his neck and flashing a distant, superior look at Su-Lin.

'You . . . you went to see Dr Sunny?' Hope flickered in Su-Lin's breast. Sunny would have recognized Dennis's state of mind, would have known that he was on the edge. And hadn't she already dropped hints to the doctor that her boyfriend was not the most stable of people? No, she forced herself to concede. She had not.

She had revealed absolutely nothing about her relationship. All she was doing now was clutching at straws.

Ignoring her question, Dennis was himself clutching at something. Forcing herself back to the reality of her plight, Su-Lin peered at him in the dim light. To her horror, she saw that Dennis was holding a cuddly toy, looking fondly into its blank glass eyes and stroking it with a tender, loving hand. She choked back a sob, willed herself not to retch, not to scream.

'All we've ever done', said Dennis in a new, conversational tone, 'is make money. Couple of kids'd make *sense* of it all.' He smiled at his partner in life. 'I distinctly remember you saying it.'

Suddenly Su-Lin was angry. She forgot her intention not to enrage him. She ignored the fact that she was bound at the wrists and ankles by Dennis's own hand. She forgot that she was a prisoner in a metal cage. 'I said that *years* ago, Dennis! You didn't *want* children.'

Dennis smiled and leaned closer again. 'I know, darling. Now I'm saying you were right.' One hand still clutching the cuddly toy, he cupped her chin in the other. 'I'm on your side. You should', he added with what seemed like genuine surprise, 'be smiling.'

Su-Lin took a deep breath. Then, with a huge effort of will, she smiled, shaking her head as she did so. 'We've got nothing to offer.' That, at least, was true.

Dennis nodded. 'Yeah. Chicken and egg, innit?' His accent was suddenly different, less refined. He didn't seem to notice. 'All my mates who've got 'em say there's never a right time. Don't you wonder', he added as he shot her a piercing, accusing look, 'what it'll look like? 'Course, I say "it" – but you might've had a scan for all I know. Do you *know* what sex it is?' Su-Lin didn't think she could take any more. Every second brought a new, lightning change in Dennis's demeanour. She was exhausted with trying to second-guess him; trying not to rile him. She lowered her head and saw, out of the corner of her eye, that Dennis's fingers, taut and white with tension, were now gripping the toy round the neck. She exhaled deeply and looked up again, meeting his questioning gaze. 'You need help,' she said.

Dennis appeared to think that was reasonable – and that he already had help. 'Yes. We've got each other. I've dipped before,' he said with his boyish grin. 'We've panicked before. We've rowed before. We always come out the other side, don't we?'

But not this time, thought Su-Lin. She looked around her, at the stark metal walls and at the pathetic supplies provided by Dennis. Fear gripped her again.

'Dennis,' she whispered, hoping her voice didn't betray her terror, 'you can't keep me here till I deliver a baby.'

'*Our* baby.'

'That's over *five months!*' she screamed. 'If you keep me here, I'll die!'

But the father-to-be was shaking his head. 'Don't be a softy. Look at me, Su-Lin.'

Fighting to control her panic, Su-Lin looked. Dennis was smiling his most disarming smile. He looked sad, and he was, she noted, fiddling with his hair. *His hair*, she suddenly thought. Why was it so important to him? Why the secrecy about dyeing it? Why the secrecy about *everything*? About his childhood? That, she knew, was unusual for an Englishman. Usually they talked of nothing else. Dennis talked about everything else but that.

Dennis was looking wounded. 'Would I hurt you?' he protested. 'Have I *ever* hurt you?'

'No' was the answer to the second question, but Su-Lin answered neither. She couldn't bring herself to contemplate the answer to the first.

Dennis looked around. Where Su-Lin had been appalled, he was admiring. 'I'll get you the other stuff you need . . . a bed . . . your books. But this', he said with an expansive wave, 'is spacious for Hong Kong. It's bigger than our first apartment. You've got space. Time to think.'

Oh God. Five months in which to think. But how many weeks, how many days before I go mad – or before Dennis decides to play a more dangerous game than happy families?

Dennis seemed to sense that her mind was elsewhere. Suddenly full of raw energy, he jumped to his feet.

'On your feet,' he said with an enthusiastic smile, 'you've got work to do, madam.' Su-Lin groaned. The cuddly toy was now forgotten. Dennis was grinning from ear to ear – and weaving the stretchband around his fingers in unconscious mockery of the way he had bound Su-Lin's hands. 'Come on,' he repeated, 'on your feet.'

Su-Lin's feet were still shackled. Dennis didn't

appear to notice. Suppressing a groan, she struggled onto her knees and then, upright and unsteady, she forced herself to smile at Dennis. He held out the stretchband. She reached for it with hands that were also bound. There was now determination in her smile, focus in her eyes. Again Dennis didn't notice: all he was interested in was the stretchband, the exercises that Su-Lin was about to perform; the health of their baby.

'Under your left foot,' he instructed. 'Round your waist . . . and s-t-r-e-t-c-h. Pull!' Eyes shining with zeal, he continued his gross parody of instruction.

Su-Lin did as she was bid. Painfully and pathetically, she tried to pull the stretchband to its limits. The more she pulled, the more her shackles restricted her.

Upset that she couldn't mimic his grotesque gestures, Dennis leaned forward and untied one of her hands, then one of her legs, smiling as he did so. Su-Lin smiled as well, but for different reasons. Careful not to make any unexpected movements, she resumed her stretching, following Dennis, obeying him. Now, able to lean and stretch further, she established a rhythm, up and down, leaning and stretching – all the time with her eyes on Dennis. She didn't need to look down again: she had spotted, when Dennis was untying her foot, the heavy juicer on the floor. She knew its position exactly; knew that each increased downward movement brought her hand ever closer to it.

Dennis was delighted with her efforts. Grinning from ear to ear, he was flailing around, matching her neat movements with his own wild ones – and dangerously off-balance every time he lunged downwards.

He was unbalanced, leaning to the left, when Su-Lin sprang. One moment he was on his feet, the next he was lying, dazed, on the floor. Su-Lin threw the juicer to the ground and, panting with exertion, scrambled towards the door. Heart pounding, she pushed at it with all her might, sobbing and gulping as she did so. Freedom was only inches away. The arc-ights illuminating the waterfront were visible now; she whimpered in a mixture of relief and desperation as she shoved one last time and began to clamber out.

And then she felt a hand grasp her ankle. She screamed, a piercing yell that echoed into the darkness as she was pulled backwards, back into her prison. Back to her confinement.

Chapter Four

Fitz had his way. He moved to the Ritz Carlton as a guest of the Royal Hong Kong Police Force. That august and – because of Peter Yang's demise – rather desperate body also agreed to his request for assistance from the UK. Jane Penhaligon would be arriving on the six o'clock flight at Kai Tak Airport. Things were definitely looking up, he thought as he looked around his spacious room with its harbour view, phones, fax machine, television, silent but deadly effective air-conditioning and luxurious *en-suite* bathroom. Janet Lee Cheung had insisted that he wait a day before moving from the Tsang Te Hotel. 'To confirm that Manchester will send Penhaligon.'

Now ensconced and with an hour to kill before meeting Jane at Kai Tak, Fitz took his revenge on Janet by savouring the delights of what for him was the greatest luxury of the room – the minibar. It was seriously well-appointed. The Ritz Carlton, Ellison had explained, was favoured by advertising types, 'especially Japanese ones'. This, to Fitz, was manna from heaven. The combination of advertising and Japanese could mean only one thing. Or, he mused as he examined the contents of what was more of a maxibar, many, many things.

'Is opportunity', he said aloud in his best Sean Connery voice, 'a weakness? Or is weakness an opportunity?' He opted, after not a great deal of deliberation, to exclude the concept of weakness altogether and concentrate on the opportunity.

As he sat on the bed sipping whisky, he looked around again and wondered how much all the luxury of the Ritz Carlton was costing the police. More, much more than the two thousand dollars per day he was getting, that was for sure. Bloody, bloody money.

Then he remembered. Judith needed money: he'd promised to wire some back to Manchester as soon as he received payment from the lecture circuit. Well, he'd received payment – and lost it on that night of illegal, impassioned gambling. That wouldn't impress Judith: it wouldn't surprise her either. She'd had twenty-two years to get used to it: twenty-two years of a marriage that had begun in heaven, flirted with hell, and then got stuck in the River Styx. But for all that had passed between them – the affairs, the separations and the wrangles over the children – it was still a marriage. Sort of.

Trying not to think of Panhandle's imminent arrival – and the room reserved for her next door – Fitz reached for the phone. Perhaps, he thought as he dialled, Katie would answer and he, the great professional expert on relationships, wouldn't have to talk to his wife.

'Judith?' The 'hello' on the other end of the line could have been from next door. Fitz's heart sank. Then, in response to the indignant squeak in his ear, it rose again. 'Oh. Katie! You sound just like your mother.' The comment, he realized too late, sounded like a reproach. 'How are you? . . . Good. Yes, I'm good too. Listen, will you tell your mother I'm sending some money tomorrow?' He cackled and rustled a fistful of dollars near the mouthpiece. 'Hear that? Tell her you heard that.'

Katie was unimpressed.

So, after another thirty seconds' conversation, was her father. Katie sounded distracted, only half-interested in talking to him. It didn't take long for Fitz to deduce that there was someone else in the room with her – and judging by the sudden giggle from her end, it wasn't her mother.

Fitz frowned. This was not good. Katie with a boyfriend. Was she *old* enough? How old were they supposed to be nowadays anyway? Another stifled giggle confirmed his suspicions. 'Who's that?' he barked. Then, on hearing his daughter's response, the worry gave way to incredulity. 'Brett? You're dating a *Brett*?' That was too much. 'Put him on! Just put him on the phone, Katie.'

But Katie had a better idea. She hung up.

Fitz stared at the receiver in his hand. Brett had been bad enough. This was nothing short of mutiny. What had happened to the well-mannered daughter he had been so proud of? The polite little girl who wouldn't say 'boo' to a goose? Fitz shook his head. Judith. It was all Judith's fault. She was spoiling Katie. Fitz replaced the receiver – and steadfastly ignored the little voice in his head. The voice was telling him that the only thing happening to Katie was that she was growing up exactly like her father.

He walked back to the minibar and poured another drink. Then, lighting an accompanying cigarette, he went over to the window. The view soothed him; lifted his mood. The greatest harbours in the world, he had heard, were Sydney, Hong Kong and Rio. Well, Sydney and Rio would have to wait for another day – another lecture? Another murder? But Hong Kong was certainly no disappointment. The hotel, on the smart parade of Connaught Road Central, next to the Hong Kong Club and a block away from the even more expensive Mandarin Hotel, was as close to the harbour as was possible. According to Freddie, twenty years previously it would have been bang on the waterfront. Twenty years, mused Fitz, looking at the rather less salubrious bus depot and the Prince of Wales Barracks built on reclaimed land. What would this place be like in another twenty years? At this rate, the sea would disappear altogether and the island would be joined to Kowloon.

He looked across the water, marvelling at the endless stream of planes swarming down to land in the impossibly positioned airport. With the runways smack on the Kowloon side of the harbour, the planes as good as landed in the middle of the city. Watching a wide-bellied jumbo make its agonizingly slow descent across the water, Fitz recalled his own arrival. The plane's wing tips had only just stopped short of whipping the washing off the racks that hung out of the high-rise windows. Fitz, by that time on his umpteenth drink and looking out of the window with barely concealed terror, had actually seen an old Chinese man calmly eating noodles on a rooftop only yards from the plane. Then a runway had appeared out of the water and the plane was on the ground, speeding towards yet more skyscrapers and endangering the lives of God only knew how many other unsuspecting residents. The passenger on his right, seeing Fitz's discomfiture, had smiled and sought to reassure him by pointing out that if they didn't stop soon enough they wouldn't crash into a building but would fall into the sea at the other end.

And now Panhandle was somewhere up there. Was she in one of the two planes circling around, awaiting clearance to land? Was she looking out of the window as he had done, wondering if her life was about to end? Or was she wondering if her relationship with Fitz was about to begin again? Was she, like him, confused?

Fitz sighed and drained his glass. He supposed he would find out soon enough about his personal relationship with Jane Penhaligon. Whatever happened there, one thing was for sure: their professional relationship was well-nigh unbeatable. The double act of interrogation that they performed was, by common consent, masterful. The only problem was, thus far, that they had no one to interrogate about the murder of Peter Yang. He wondered if Janet Lee Cheung had got any further with her investigations. Fitz looked again at the planes overhead and then at his watch. Time, he reckoned, to get a taxi to the airport. Time to find out about Panhandle.

As previously arranged, Janet joined him at Kai Tak. Her innate air of authority, rather than her ID, saw them both escorted to the British Airways first-class lounge. Fitz ordered a drink. Janet looked disapproving. Fitz ignored her and ambled over to the huge plate-glass window to watch the activity above and below. Janet finally aired her worries.

'I don't want personal relationships', she said, 'screwing up my investigation.'

Fitz, still at the window, had his back to her. He sensed, rather than saw, her defensively crossed legs and disdainful expression. She couldn't see his grin.

When he turned to face her, the grin had been replaced by a cryptic smile. 'Coming from another female detective,' he retorted, 'might I suggest it's a trifle narrow-minded and slightly ironic to assume it's personal?'

'You've specifically asked for her to be put in a connecting room to yours.'

Touché, thought Fitz. And I hope your groundwork on the Yang case has been equally thorough. He inclined his head very slightly. 'Ah! Yes. I suppose I have.'

But Janet wasn't amused. 'You're costing me a lot of

money. I am not paying for a honeymoon.'

And some marriages, thought Fitz, end on the honeymoon. Or even before. Was this all a terrible mistake, he wondered? Was it even strictly necessary? Then, still without replying, he smiled to himself. It was probably nothing more than a bad attack of airport arrival nerves. Even he, consummate manipulator and expert conversationalist, became tongue-tied in the role of airport-greeter. *Did you have a nice flight? Did they bump you up to first? You'll soon get used to the heat. Will you sleep with me tonight?* What was he going to say to her? But before he could respond to Janet's jibe, the lounge attendant approached and informed them that Flight BA109 had landed. They repaired in silence to Arrivals.

Jane Penhaligon hadn't been bumped up to first class. She wasn't amongst the first passengers to come through Customs. Nor was she amongst those with 'club' stickers on their luggage. Fitz looked sidelong at Janet. So, despite the fact that she knew the new arrival would have to hit the ground running, she had only stumped up for an economy fare. Fitz closed his eyes and conjured up a picture of Panhandle; more specifically, of her legs. They were shapely and elegant. They were nimble. But were they short enough to fold comfortably in a small, cramped seat? Fitz wasn't sure. Poor Panhandle.

Then he opened his eyes again and very nearly had a heart attack. In panic, he closed them again. The sight before him was merely a nasty trick of his imagination. He was having a nightmare. But when he summoned the courage to look again he discovered the nightmare was real. Standing in front of him, bearded, portly and extremely rumpled, was Detective Chief Inspector Charlie Wise, Panhandle's boss. 'Oh Jesus,' he whispered. 'No!'

'Aye, aye,' called Wise as, adjusting his glasses, he spotted Fitz. Hand luggage in one hand, duty free in the other, he shuffled up to them.

But Fitz had turned to stone. 'Where', he said without moving a muscle to greet Wise, 'is she?'

Wise chuckled. 'I didn't know spouses were invited,' he said in his broad Mancunian accent. 'Reenie'd have loved that flight, I'll tell you now.' He shook his head, still dazed by his first ever long-haul flight. 'Talk about the eye of a bloody needle.' Then, seeing that Fitz was still gawping like a dead fish, he extended a hand to Janet. 'Detective Chief Inspector Wise. Greater Manchester Police. How you doing, love?'

'Love' was doing rather well, and especially enjoying Fitz's total shock. She wasn't, however, so sure about being called 'love'. Was it patronizing, or just the way they spoke in Manchester? It would be difficult to be this man's love. His dark hair was too long, his glasses were unfashionable and he was too short for her taste in Englishmen. Yet he seemed amiable enough and, more to the point, was having a catastrophic effect on Fitz. She smiled, shook hands, and introduced herself. Wise then turned back to Fitz. He seemed completely unaware that the psychologist was reeling from shock. 'Reenie wants a windchime,' he said. 'Whatever I do before I go home,' he added as he wagged a finger in front of Fitz, 'remind me. *Windchime* – or I'm a dead man.'

Fitz suddenly came alive. '*Penhaligon! Where the hell's Penhaligon?*'

'Oh. Didn't you know? She's just been made up to Inspector.' Wise chuckled. 'She's back at school. The Home Office asked for a senior officer. I'm the only one with holidays left.' Then, serious now, he turned back to Janet. 'Didn't you get the message?'

Fitz also turned to the policewoman. Her smile said it all. Yes, she had got the message. No, she deliberately hadn't told Fitz. And she had, with equal deliberation, been trying to pry into Fitz's love life. Grinning, she turned and, with a friendly arm on Wise's elbow, indicated for him to follow her. Fitz she left to his own devices.

'I hope you don't mind,' she said in a voice loud enough for Fitz to hear, 'but we've put you in a room next to Dr Fitzgerald.'

Behind her, Dr Fitzgerald muttered a string of obscenities.

Wise began to sweat as they left the air-conditioned cool of the airport. 'This is nothing,' said Fitz unkindly. 'Heat of the day's much worse. Humidity's knackering.'

Janet glared at him and unlocked the car.

'I never thought', said Wise as he leaned back with a sigh of relief in the passenger seat, 'that we'd make it.'

'Oh? Bad flight?'

Wise shook his head and gestured towards the runway

appearing on their left. 'No. *That*. I mean, *look* at it.'

Janet laughed. 'Yes. Everyone says that. It's pretty spectacular, isn't it? But not that many planes topple into the sea.'

'You're joking?'

'No. But they're usually Dragon Air planes. Nothing for you to worry about.'

'Oh. Well that's all right then, isn't it?' Feeling anything but all right, Wise looked away from the airport. Skyscrapers. Motorways. Water. Lots of little rocky outcrops and that bloody great hill they had nearly hit. He didn't know why, but he had assumed Hong Kong would be flat. He grimaced as Janet accelerated into the midst of lanes of thundering traffic.

'Furthest I've been is Fuengirola,' he explained. 'Bit different.' Then he extracted a grubby handkerchief from his pocket and wiped his face. 'God, look at me, sweating like a pig already. I hear', he added suddenly, 'that coppers're on really good money here. Is that right, love?'

But Janet didn't have an opportunity to reply. Her car phone rang and, with a brief smile of apology to Wise, she reached forward to answer it. Wise was rather taken aback by the fact that she answered in Cantonese. Behind him, Fitz was more interested in her body language. She tensed as she listened; her knuckles turned white on the steering-wheel. Then she replaced the phone and turned to Wise. 'I hope you're ready for action. There's been another murder.'

'What?'

'Yes.' She met Fitz's eyes in the rear-view mirror and nodded.

Wise seemed almost pleased.

'Yeah,' he said, straightening his lapels. 'I'm wide awake now. Ready for anything.' But not, it later turned out, for the sight of Dr Sunny.

Behind him, Fitz was thrown against the back seat as Janet activated her siren and accelerated into the traffic. 'Another murder', in this context, could only mean one thing: another killing by the same person. Why else would Janet, and not another senior officer, be informed? Fitz wasn't exactly pleased – but he did feel vindicated in demanding back-up from the UK. Even if it was in the unprepossessing shape of DCI Charlie Wise.

Two hours later, Wise was drained to the point of exhaustion. Fourteen hours in the air; bad food; too much alcohol, and then a mad dash across Hong Kong; the grotesque sight of a dead man pinned to a car tyre by a knife through his throat: all had taken their toll. But it had been the grotesque sight of the dead man pinned to a car tyre that had really finished him.

And now here he was, battling fatigue, feeling distinctly grubby, and sitting at a conference table at the headquarters of the Royal Hong Kong Police Force. He was still sufficiently alert to notice that this building – outside and in – was a far cry from the dingy, dilapidated Victoriana of Anson Road HQ in Manchester. The police officers, however, were not so different. They were in complete disagreement with each other.

Making use of the silence while a junior detective pinned some forensic photographs on the noticeboard, Wise looked around. The man who had been introduced to him as Commander Gordon Ellison was trying his best not to look bored. He was also trying his utmost not to be seen to agree with anyone, to take sides. Wise correctly surmised that the man would rather be at home sipping a cool gin and tonic.

On either side of him sat Janet Lee Cheung and Fitz. Both were tight-lipped; Janet was slightly flushed; Fitz looked mutinous. If nothing else, Ellison was performing a valuable service by separating them.

The junior detective finished his task and resumed his place opposite Wise. Everyone looked at the photos on the board. There were head shots, hand shots, scene-of-crime shots and murder weapon shots. The methods of killing were patently different – but there was one unmistakable similarity.

Janet turned back to her colleagues. 'We have to treat these as two separate murders.'

Irritated, Fitz sighed heavily and shook his head. Janet ignored him.

'The first body', she continued, 'was killed with a blunt instrument.' She pointed to the photograph of the Jockey Club Trophy. 'The second was knifed. The first was killed in a private office, the second in a public place.'

Fitz shook his head again and pointed to the photographs of the dead men's hands. 'But they both had their hands tied, *specifically* like this.'

Janet wasn't impressed. 'I don't see why that's specific. How else do you secure a victim?'

Fitz's expression showed that he could think of many other ways.

He looked briefly at the notes in front of him and then back at Janet. 'The pathologist questions whether the hands were tied before or after death. I'm saying it happened after. He left both bodies in a state of disgrace. He killed them in the dark. Left them with their heads bowed. That', he finished, 'is not accidental.'

Janet was openly scathing. 'I don't know how many dead people you've seen, Dr Fitzgerald, but they all tend to look like that.'

Wise, while still alive, was also beginning to look like that. His head kept nodding forward; each time he managed to nudge himself into life, it was with less conviction, less enthusiasm. Only Ellison noticed. The others were too busy arguing.

The junior detective, Benny Ho, was plainly on Janet's side. 'The face of Peter Yang was covered,' he said. 'Dr Sunny's wasn't.'

Fitz waved a dismissive hand. 'Dr Sunny', he countered, 'was left sunny side up because the murderer had no shame in killing him. Either he'd never met this guy before or he's simply losing his conscience. The *emotional* and *behavioural* hallmarks of both murders are identical. It was a different weapon because you've got the first in a bloody forensics lab. The point is,' he continued, banging an authoritative fist on the table, 'he *came with a weapon* the second time. He's shifted from being a "man who killed" to "a killer". More confident, organized, harder to catch. And he conducts ritual humiliation: "You are more powerful than me. I can't do anything about that, but if I take your life, I win."'

Janet was sceptical, both of Fitz's conclusion and of the paucity of information he had to arrive at it. She was used to hard facts, not high-flown theories. 'And you're saying that's his only motive?'

'Absolutely.'

Janet was grinning now. She knew otherwise. Imitating Fitz, she tapped the table with a fist. 'Fact: Dr Sunny was carrying ten thousand dollars when he left his office. His secretary saw him pack it in his briefcase. Fact: only three and a half thousand remained. In the absence of further evidence, we treat the killing of Dr Sunny as Aggravated Robbery with Homicide. And we think the killer was disturbed – there must be witnesses.' Then, with a 'challenge me if you dare' expression, she glared at Fitz.

Fitz, however, couldn't even be bothered to challenge her. She was making it plain that she considered criminal psychology was a load of bunkum. Fine, let her, he thought. But why bother keeping him on board? Why fly Wise over? Fitz looked at Ellison. The senior policeman was looking uncomfortable, even a little sheepish – yet he made no attempt to challenge Janet. Fitz stood up, as if to leave the room. Then he clasped his hands together in the manner of the dead men. 'And this', he said to Janet, 'means nothing?'

Janet didn't have an answer to that one, didn't want

to admit that there were, in fact, other ways to bind a victim.

'A prayer, maybe?' Fitz could have been talking to a small child. 'Praying?' Then, taking everyone by surprise, he turned again to Ellison. 'What're you? C of E? Methodist?'

'C of E – but only when I go to hospital.' Nobody laughed. 'You?' he added with a sudden seriousness.

'Catholic.' Fitz grinned. 'But only when I go into a bookie's.' Keeping his hands together, he raised them and closed his eyes. 'Hail Mary, Mother of God, pray for us winners now and at the hour of our death.' The gesture carried an air of desperation and the words, despite their deliberate jocularity, seemed somehow powerful. Then, opening his eyes, still consumed with passion, he looked at Janet. 'That's a *Christian* symbol. A *western* gesture.'

Janet frowned. 'So what?' was the reply she nearly made. But instead she bit her lip – and the doubt flickered in her eyes.

Fitz noticed it; saw second thoughts registering; the questioning look she then gave to Ellison. He ignored her hesitation and, seizing his moment, turned to Benny Ho. 'How many people have you interviewed so far?'

'Forty.' Benny beamed with pride.

'How many westerners?'

'Um . . . well . . .' Benny consulted his notes. 'Well, none . . . no, one . . .'

'You've been looking in the wrong place. The killer of these men', said Fitz with absolute conviction, 'is not Chinese. He's white. Western. Caucasian.' He turned to

Janet. 'He's an outsider.'

Again Janet looked to Ellison. Ellison tried a tentative smile and looked at Wise. Wise looked half-dead, yet the sudden smile he gave Fitz indicated that at least part of his brain was attuned to what was happening.

'He *lives* here,' continued Fitz. 'He's not a visitor because he knew his way around Peter Yang's diary. He knew the man worked late and would be in the office at night. He also knew the layout of the office. Ergo, he knew Yang. And', he said as he banged his fist again, 'he's a *loser* because he yearns for power but doesn't have any. The only reason', he asked his now captive audience, 'he trashed the office; broke the glass?'

'To protect his identity.' Everyone turned, slightly alarmed, to Wise. They had forgotten he could speak.

'Correct.'

'Which means', said Wise as he pulled himself straight in his chair, 'that he could be traced back to his victim.'

Fitz paused for a moment and then turned back to Janet. He smiled an 'I'm too polite to call you a half-wit' smile. 'That narrow the field down for you?'

Wise didn't remember much after that. The meeting drew to an abrupt close, he was somehow transported to a hotel and the last thing he remembered – apart from Reenie's request for a windchime – was watching a Cantonese soap opera from the vantage point of a very large and extremely luxurious bed.

Chapter Five

Janet was so annoyed by Fitz's behaviour, so humiliated by his deliberately patronizing manner, that she spent half the night and all the next morning researching Peter Yang's western contacts. She hadn't been able to end that awful meeting soon enough; she had very nearly hit Fitz, and she had taken her anger out, unfairly, on the hapless Benny Ho. It wasn't until later, as she sat alone in her office faxing requests to Revenue Tower about Yang's income and expenditure, that she conceded she was partly to blame for Fitz's high-handed manner. She knew she had made no bones about the fact that she regarded him as an unnecessary complication; as a nuisance who believed in words rather than action. She knew she had invited his derision by treating him with her own disdain. Yet that didn't alter the fact that he had shown himself to be an arrogant bastard even before they had started working together. When she cast her mind back to her first encounter with him in the university bar, her lip still curled in distaste. She disliked him even more now that he had made her look a fool.

Janet was not a fool. She was highly intelligent, highly motivated – and extremely apprehensive. Like so many Hong Kong Chinese, she had no idea what the future held in store for her. And like so many Hong Kong Chinese, she had laboured long and hard under British rule – yet was denied a British passport. People like Fitz, she knew, assumed that she couldn't wait to see the back of the British, to see her homeland revert to China. The former was true; she had no love for the British and their high-handed way of doing business. She had been discriminated against in her career because of them – until they had started running scared and had begun to promote the Chinese within their ranks. Now, of course, there were very few British left in the police force: very few Ellisons around. And that, as far as Janet was concerned, was a very good thing indeed. She couldn't bear Ellison.

But the larger problem was no longer the British. The problem was the Chinese. She was no more one of them than she was British. Even people like Ellison who had lived in Hong Kong for years assumed that, because she looked like 'them', she was one of them and understood them. Well, she wasn't and she didn't. And while she had been assured that 'nothing would change' after the handover, she couldn't be certain. That was why her career was so important to her. She wanted to be seen to be indispensable. And the maintenance of law and order was, even after 1997, going to be an integral part of Hong Kong's future success in the international marketplace. Janet wanted to be part of it.

So, despite her personal feelings, she took Fitz's comments extremely seriously. At two in the morning, she left police headquarters secure in the knowledge that she now had a suspect for Peter Yang's murder. A westerner. A Christian. Someone who had known Peter Yang very well and for many years. A foreigner familiar with Hong Kong. Her information had been hard to come by: it was almost as if Yang's lawyers and his widow didn't want the murder solved. Their protectiveness bordered on paranoia. But Janet could, to a large extent, understand that. Peter Yang, in getting himself murdered, had lost face. He had brought shame on his family. And that family was now in a most peculiar position: solving the murder was, of course, desirable – yet the story behind it might turn out to heap further disgrace on the family.

Investigating the death of Dr Sunny should, Janet hoped, present fewer difficulties. The man had had a lower profile and status; he was of no interest to the business or social communities. There would be no obstacles in the way, no army of legal experts to descend and cover his tracks. With any luck, Dr Sunny's secretary would be able to reveal, in the morning, the names of every patient he had seen over the past few weeks, months or even years.

But what, Janet asked herself as she drove back to

spend yet another night alone, was the connection between the businessman and the doctor. What linked them, and why? Sunny, she knew from her preliminary research, was known to 'deal' with pregnancies. The thought made her want to retch. She dismissed it. No; there had to be something else, some sort of clandestine activity that linked the two men – and some way they had both managed to cross their killer.

Janet went to bed the minute she got home. Sleep did not elude her, but relaxation did. She tossed and turned; she sweated in the cool of the night; her eyes flickered and raced beneath her closed lids, and she moaned in terror as she was beset by visions of her hands being bound in prayer while her life was extinguished by a madman.

Janet took Fitz and Charlie Wise to meet her suspect the following afternoon. She had spent the morning verifying his association with Peter Yang's business – and trying to get a lead on Dr Sunny's extra-medical activities. She failed in the latter quest. There had never been a complaint filed against the doctor; the only club the man appeared to belong to was the exclusive Shek-O Golf Club; he was happily married; there was no hint of any other, clandestine relationship, and he appeared to spend most of his time working or playing golf. Not, in short, the sort of person to go and get himself murdered. Had it not been for the prayer-like position of the bound hands, Janet would have sworn his death had nothing in common with Peter Yang's. But the more she thought about the hands, the more she knew that Fitz was right: the killer was one and the same person. A copy-cat killing was unlikely – not to say impossible. Apart from the very short space of time between the two killings, one vital piece of information had been kept from the public about the manner of Yang's death: Janet had not released the information about the hands.

Janet left a message at the Ritz Carlton for Fitz and Wise to meet her in the foyer of her suspect's office building in Wanchai, a mere two blocks from the hotel. She had not requested that they spend the morning with her at head-quarters: they had not offered to do so. She had assumed Wise would want to sleep off his jet lag. Fitz, no doubt, would be sleeping off a hangover. She knew him well enough to deduce that he would have one: not well enough to know that he would never admit to having one, let alone succumbing to it.

She saw Wise the moment she stepped into the cool atrium of the building. He was wearing yesterday's crumpled suit, yesterday's lugubrious expression – and he was carrying a particularly gaudy windchime.

'Hello, love,' he said as he waved the tinkling monstrosity at her. 'All set, then?' He looked around, admiring of the massive glass and steel chandeliers, the acres of marble, the hushed atmosphere and the uniformed attendants. 'This is where our man works?'

Janet nodded, both in agreement and in acknowledgement of Fitz, appearing behind Wise. Then she looked, very pointedly, at the windchime. 'Perhaps they could keep it at the desk for you? We don't want to . . . to . . .'

'Create the wrong impression?' finished Fitz for her.

Janet smiled thinly. She could already tell he wasn't convinced by the trail they were following. Suddenly it made her angry. What the hell did he have to be so superior about, anyway? She was doing all the leg-work: all he had done so far was scoff at her results.

He showed his scepticism when, two minutes after depositing the windchime at the enquiries desk, they emerged from the lift on the twenty-third floor. The reception area was even more plush, dripped even more money than the atrium below. It was considerably more garish. Fitz pursed his lips as he took in the faux-leopardskin sofa, the intricately carved table and the profusion of crystal artefacts and chandeliers. Only a discreet sign above the reception desk in the corner told them that this was not a tart's boudoir but the headquarters of Carter Exports. The receptionist, decorated with the same attention to overkill, informed them that she was terribly sorry but that Mr Carter was, in fact, not in his office.

'Not here?' Fitz glared at her. 'What do you mean "not here"?'

The receptionist glared back. 'He's been detained at home. But he did phone to say', she added with a bountiful smile, 'that he would be happy to receive you there.'

'Oh great.' Fitz rolled his eyes. 'And where exactly might home be?'

The receptionist looked smug. 'The Peak.'

*

Neither Fitz nor Janet said a word during the journey. Reunited with the windchime and in the back of Janet's car, Wise admired the view as they climbed. Janet seethed silently at the wheel. Bloody man, she thought over and over again. Then, catching Fitz's expression out of the corner of her eye, she changed that to bloody men. Fitz was pleased Frank Carter hadn't been in his office. And his silence was more eloquent than any words. *You've got the wrong man*, it said. Anyone who treats the police in such a cavalier fashion has nothing to worry about. And anyone with an office decorated like Carter's has absolutely nothing to hide.

Fitz didn't articulate his thoughts until, almost at the summit of the Peak, they turned through an ornate wrought-iron gateway and into a short, well-maintained driveway. 'Hmm,' he said. 'Nice.' The tone of his voice implied the opposite; very nasty indeed. And then, as they drove past the well-manicured flowerbeds and pulled up in front of an even nastier house, he turned and smiled at Janet. 'Wrong,' he said. 'A man with a house like this – and this far up the Peak – is anything but an underachiever.'

Janet didn't reply. Tight-lipped, she turned off the engine, opened her door and leaped out of the vehicle. She knew that Fitz was right: she had known it the minute she had seen the address the receptionist had written down for them. Anyone who lived a stone's throw from the residence of the Governor of the Hong Kong and Shanghai Bank was not down on their luck. Anyone who bought or built a house like this had more money than they knew what to do with – and certainly more money than taste. Janet walked towards the huge mahogany front door, wrinkling her nose at the caryatids above the triple garage; at the cupids gambolling on the roof of the mock-Tudor conservatory and at the brightly painted cartwheels propped against the hacienda-style loggia. No, she thought, Frank Carter was not their man. But that didn't mean defeat; didn't merit Fitz's supercilious sneer. Frank Carter might not be guilty – but he might know who was.

A manservant opened the door a mere fraction of a second after Janet rang the bell. Without a word, yet somehow managing to convey an innate superiority, he gestured for the visitors to follow him into the house. As she stalked into the building, Janet was suddenly glad that Fitz and Wise were behind her and that they couldn't see her expression. The rooms they passed through would have made a brothel-keeper blush. They were beyond bad taste; beyond a joke.

But there was nothing funny about the man waiting for them on the terrace. Neither the perfectly capped teeth nor the overblown Versace shirt – nor even the smile that failed to reach his eyes – could disguise the fact that Frank Carter was a wide-boy. An ageing wide-boy wearing a veneer of sophistication – but a wide-boy nonetheless. And a chauvinist.

'Gentlemen,' he boomed, ignoring Janet and making a bee-line for Fitz and Wise. 'Frank Carter. How you doin'?'

Wise shook the proffered hand. 'Wise,' he said,

dispensing with his title. Then, grinning, he pointed to the stony-faced Janet. 'And meet the boss, DCI Cheung.'

Poised to greet 'the boss' in the form of Fitz, Carter looked distinctly put out. 'Ah. Yeah.' Clasping Janet's hand in a perfunctory way, he gestured for them to sit at the table. But that gesture was equally perfunctory, somehow robbing them of any pleasure they might have derived from the breath-taking panoramic view of Hong Kong. 'I'm due at the airport by half-past,' he suddenly remembered. 'You've got ten minutes.'

Fifty, thought Fitz. He'd be about fifty. The tan is fake: this man spends all his time indoors. The shirt is real: flamboyant, multicoloured and made of silk. And it screams 'look at me – but don't try to use me'. A bit like Carter.

'So,' said the businessman, smiling in a vaguely patronizing way and making a pyramid of his hands under his chin, 'you're here about Peter Yang? Nasty business. Really nasty.' The words were addressed to Fitz: the prayer-like position of the hands completely natural. Fitz smiled back. If he needed any confirmation that Carter was not their man, then that was it. Only a very clever or a very stupid murderer would flaunt his trademark in front of the police. Carter was neither. Nor was he a murderer: the act of killing could be a messy one. Blood might spill on the shirt. Or the socks. Fitz had gleaned enough about designer clothes in the last few days to recognize the little elephants for what they were: Hermès.

'Yes . . .' began Fitz.

'We're conducting preliminary inquiries', interrupted Janet, 'amongst his business associates . . .'

Carter laughed, a great bellow of amusement, straight from the East End of London. 'You don't think I killed him, do you, lovey?'

Janet bridled. Would he call Fitz 'lovey'? No. 'We're not in a position', she continued with an acid look across the table, 'to rule out anyone or anything. However,' she added, pre-empting Fitz, 'we'd appreciate it if you could provide us with the names of any of Yang's contacts you might know.'

'Can't his own business do that?' The question wasn't stalling or defensive; more mildly interested, slightly surprised.

'Yang's lawyers are doing all they can, but we're . . .'

'Yeah, I see.' Carter nodded at Janet. He *did* see. Yang's lawyers would be throwing every obstacle they could at the police. They would be co-operating as little as possible. Being secretive. Carter knew all about that. Carter liked that.

Janet didn't bother to complete her sentence, to say they were 'exploring every avenue'. She knew that Carter knew what clout the might of Yang Associates could wield – even in the face of the police.

'Well,' said Carter, leaning back in his seat, 'our relationship was latterly more *social* than professional . . .'

'. . . So you wouldn't know if he had latterly become a little *unscrupulous?*' Fitz smiled at Carter, but his eyes were mocking.

Carter immediately regretted his line of social one-upmanship. Why even bother trying to impress these people with tales of parties on the Peak, of an exalted social milieu to which they could never aspire? They were, after all, only policemen. They had no money. 'No,' he said. 'There's no way he could have changed. Absolutely not. Yang did everything by the book.'

'Do you know a Dr Sunny?' asked Fitz suddenly.

'No.' Carter looked surprised. 'Should I?'

'Not necessarily,' said Fitz, dismissing the subject. Carter, he had already decided, would make a rotten liar. He had obviously never heard of the man – or of his murder. 'Have you any idea', he asked, 'who Yang might have been doing things by the book with? Latterly?'

Carter glared at Fitz. 'Yeah,' he said, plucking a gold fountain pen from his shirt pocket and reaching for the pad in front of him. 'I can't claim to know all his contacts, but their social life was pretty well entwined with their business.'

'Their?'

'Yeah. Peter and Nancy.' Carter smiled at Janet, deciding rather late in the proceedings that she was easier to deal with than Fitz. 'Nancy claimed to know nothing about the business, but that was just a front. A very astute woman, Peter's wife. She was in on a lot of the decisions, y'know.' Carter looked suddenly sad, for the first time revealing something of his friendship with the Yangs. 'I'm very fond of Nancy – as I was of Peter. A great man.'

'And an honest one?'

'Yes.' Carter spat out the word, not even looking at

the belligerent Scotsman to whom it was directed. Instead, he busied himself with his pen and paper. 'He worked hard,' he said as he paused mid-flow. 'That's hardly a crime, is it?' Then he smiled to himself. 'Only slept about six hours a night, but the joke was that Peter Yang did some of his best business with his eyes shut. Pure instinct,' he sighed. 'Peter just made massive amounts of money.'

Carter, noted Fitz, was admiring of that. Even perhaps a touch jealous: but not consumed by an overpowering envy. For all his bluster, Carter was probably a decent man; and a very clever operator.

'Making money is one thing the Chinese ...' suddenly Carter remembered Janet and looked up at her with an apologetic smile. 'Forgive me ... but it's one thing the Chinese have a genuine respect for, thank God.' Again the appreciation, the admiration.

'That', he said as he handed his list to Janet, 'is all the names I can think of at short notice.'

'Will you be staying, Frank?' asked Fitz suddenly.

'I'm sorry?'

'After the handover? Will you be staying where the money is, or will you be going *home*?'

Carter took that as the blatant affront it was meant to be. Then he remembered that this man was only a policeman. 'We're relocating the head office in Singapore,' he said with a condescending smile. 'We'd rather not, but', he spread his hands in front of him, 'it makes sense. Nobody, you see, knows exactly what's going to happen.'

122

Suddenly liking the man, Janet nodded in involuntary agreement. She knew that Frank Carter had spent twenty-five years in Hong Kong. It *was* home. But then Fitz wouldn't understand that.

Still with his withering gaze on Fitz, Carter stood up. 'You've had fifteen minutes.' Then he nodded towards the silent and unprepossessing-looking Wise. 'And miladdo here needs some deodorant.'

Touché, thought Janet, biting back a grin. No wonder he likes to play one-upmanship: it must be very addictive if you win all the time.

They were silent as they drove down from the Peak. Janet was perusing her list of names. Wise was wondering where he could buy deodorant, and Fitz was fuming inside. Hong Kong, he realized, was doing something unpleasant to him: it made him feel humble. The more he struck out at the people or the place, the harder the return blow. The buildings dwarfed him: the ostentatious wealth mocked him and the heat and frenetic pace exhausted him. But worst of all was the fact that he knew he hadn't cracked what lay beneath the surface of the place. Only the temporary seemed permanent. Nothing and nobody was rooted. Suddenly he remembered his trip to the botanical gardens and the notice beside a flower that was strange to him. '*Bauhinia*', it had read. '*The national flower of Hong Kong. A sterile hybrid which produces no seed.*'

'The only name on this list that we don't know', said

Janet as they reached Central, 'is someone called Dennis Philby.'

'Ah,' said Fitz, perking up. 'A westerner.'

'Can't be sure,' said Wise, anxious to re-assert his authority. 'All the Chinese seem to have western names. The girl who looked after Carter's office building', he said, brandishing the windchime, 'was called Dolly.'

'How d'you know that?'

Wise turned to Fitz. 'Her name-tag.'

'Oh.'

'Most English-speaking Chinese people here', explained Janet, 'have two Christian names. A Cantonese one and an English one.'

'Why?' asked Fitz.

Janet shrugged. 'To make the English feel better?'

Neither man responded.

'So, who', said Wise after a moment, 'is this Dennis Philby?'

Janet consulted Frank Carter's flamboyant scrawl. 'Philby Medical. Packagers of pharmaceuticals, it appears.' Then she peered at what Carter had written in brackets beside the name: 'Professional – definitely not social. Still in business???'

She showed the paper to Fitz.

'Hmm. So,' he said as he gestured towards the haze-shrouded Peak behind them, 'not admitted to parties up there. Not in the same social orbit as Yang and Carter. And yes,' he added as he saw Wise's expression, 'I know Carter's social credentials wouldn't get him through the door in England – but here it's not class but . . .'

'Money. Yes, I know that.' Janet waved a dismissive hand. 'But our man was known to both Yang and Sunny, yet Carter obviously knows precious little about Philby – apart from the fact that he's *definitely* not in the same bracket.'

'A fact', said Wise, 'of which Philby himself was no doubt aware?'

'Exactly. And', continued Fitz as he looked again at the paper, 'Carter dismisses Philby with a casual "still in business?" – suggesting that it makes no odds to anyone whether he is or not. If Philby is at all conscious of his standing in Hong Kong – and God knows everybody else seems obsessed by their own – then he knows he's regarded as a "little man".'

'An *under*achiever.'

'Yes.' Fitz looked at Janet, wondering if she was being sarcastic. Somewhat to his surprise, she looked deadly serious, even a little excited.

She was also determined not to waste any time. Reaching forward to the dashboard, she picked up her mobile and called HQ. Her two companions remained silent as she talked animatedly and in Cantonese to someone on the other end. Fitz's face was blank, betraying no hint that, yet again, he felt he was being cut down to size. Another language; another world. His only consolation was that body language was the same the world over. He deduced from Janet's expression and stance that she was merely issuing orders to someone.

'Detective Ho', she said as she retracted the receiver a moment later, 'is going to find out the address of Philby

Medical. Might as well', she added, 'strike while the iron's hot.'

'Er . . . ' Wise pointed to his windchime.

Janet grinned. 'You can store it in the boot. And, er . . . if you want to buy some deodorant, there's a shop just round the corner . . .?'

Wise wasn't sure whether she was being offensive or helpful. He decided, for the greater good of all, to give her the benefit of the doubt. 'Oh. Yes . . . that would be, um . . . nice.' He turned, grinning, to the scowling Fitz. Fitz recognized the look in Wise's eyes: 'If I can establish a rapport with this woman, then why can't you?' Wise was telling him to accept the olive branch Janet had just extended. Fitz glared back. Nobody told him what to do: he was perfectly capable of grasping the branch on his own. If and when he wanted to.

Ten minutes and two cans of deodorant later, they were back in the police station. Benny Ho had not been idle. 'Philby Medical', he said as they approached his desk, 'is still in business – and not far from here. Yang's people', he added with a broad smile, 'are familiar with Philby. They did a lot of business together. And Yang wrote Philby a cheque the day before he was murdered.'

'Hardly', said Fitz, 'a reason for killing him, is it?'

Benny Ho shrugged. 'Stranger things have happened.'

'Depends', drawled Fitz, forgetting the encouragement to amnesty, 'whether or not you're at sea, I suppose.'

'Mr Philby?' Fiona Chang's voice was less harsh today, as

indeed it had been over the past few days. She had begun to feel sorry for her boss. He had taken the news of Peter Yang's death extremely badly indeed. It was, she guessed, a brutal reminder that Philby Medical's best client would call no more.

And now this. 'The . . . the, er, police would like to talk to you.'

'To me?' Dennis's voice, betraying surprise but not panic, came back through the intercom on Fiona's desk. 'Oh. Well, send 'em in.'

Fiona clicked off the intercom and smiled up at her visitors. Dennis, alone in his office upstairs, also smiled. Several emotions had gripped him over the past few minutes. The first, when he had looked out of the window to see four strangers emerging from a car, was interest. New clients, perhaps? Just as well that he was wearing clean clothes and a newly pressed suit. Then, when he had noticed the woman take some sort of little wallet out of her pocket and flash it at the supervisor below, he had been consumed by gut-wrenching panic. He knew that gesture: it was the same the world over. Police. *Hide*, he thought.

Then he had looked around the tiny office. Hiding was out of the question. He grabbed his letter-opener with shaking hands. Not sharp enough. Then he looked at the paperweight on his desk. Not heavy enough. His scared eyes darted from one object to another in the tiny room. Nothing. There was no way he could kill himself. Then, catching sight of himself in the small mirror opposite his desk, he smiled. At first the smile was hesitant, a

127

sort of experiment to see if he could still execute such a mundane task. He could. The smile impressed him. It made him look charming, confident.

By the time Fiona buzzed on the intercom he had adjusted his tie, combed his hair, and assumed an equally confident yet relaxed stance. And by the time she ushered Fitz, Janet and Wise into his office, he was standing again at the internal window, looking benignly at his work-force in the loading bay below.

He turned as the visitors entered. There was, thought Fitz, a slight wariness about his clear blue eyes. Yet he would have been suspicious if there hadn't been. Only the very guilty or the very naïve greeted unannounced policemen with open arms and a twinkle in their eyes. Philby appeared, at first sight, to be neither. He had good features, an intelligent face, nicely cut blond hair. A well-cut shirt and a discreet tie. And his smile, when it came, was disarming.

'Dennis Philby,' he said in a well-modulated, near-accentless voice. 'Please,' he added, indicating the chairs that Fiona Chang was drawing up at the other side of his desk.

His visitors introduced themselves, shook hands, and sat down. They stared, three against one, across the table. Dennis merely raised an eyebrow.

'We're sorry to descend on you like this,' began Janet, 'but we gather you knew Peter Yang.' The blunt announcement carried no trace of accusation. Neither did it have any warmth, or even a hint of hushed reverence for the dead. It was just a statement.

'Yes,' said Dennis. 'I do . . . did. He was one of my best clients.' His tone matched Janet's. Businesslike. Betraying nothing.

'And you know he was murdered three days ago?'

'Yes.' Dennis looked, slightly patronizing, at Fitz. 'I would imagine all Hong Kong knows. Peter was something of a legend here. It's appalling,' he added, looking away. Then he turned to Janet. 'Triads?' he ventured.

'We were rather hoping', she answered, 'that *you* might be able to enlighten *us*.'

'Oh. So it's still a mystery, then?'

'We're following', said Janet, 'every possible lead.'

'Oh. Right. Well.' Dennis began to fiddle with a pen. 'So, how can I help you?'

'How long', asked Fitz, 'had you known Peter Yang?'

'Gosh . . . 'bout ten years. Twelve?'

'And how long have you lived in Hong Kong?'

'Same.'

'So you know lots of Yang's business associates?'

'No. Not really. We tended to do business on a one-to-one basis. You know, without any middle men. If it's of any use,' said Dennis, standing up and walking towards the filing cabinet below the window, 'I've got records going back years. I don't *think* they'll tell you much, but . . .' Trailing off into silence, he opened the top drawer and extracted a thick, buff file. Then he turned, charmingly hesitant, and held it out. 'Er . . . who . . .?'

Smiling her thanks, Janet stretched forward and took the file.

Fitz was beginning to wonder if Dennis Philby was

rather *too* anxious to please. Then again, he could just be a smarmy git. He was beginning to look like one.

The smarmy git smiled across the table at Fitz. 'Peter was a brilliant man, you know. I'll miss him.'

'And his money.'

Dennis flushed. He looked, extremely disapproving, at the rude Scotsman opposite him. Fat and gone to seed, he thought. Bitter, no doubt – and obsessed by money. The thought made Dennis feel suddenly uncomfortable. 'Well . . . yes, he *was* my best customer, but this is hardly the time . . . Anyway,' he added, shifting in his seat and reaching for a cigarette, 'Yang Associates will still operate. It's a huge business, you know.' His meaning was implicit in the smile he bestowed on Fitz: Yang Associates would still operate – and do business with Philby Medical.

'But Peter Yang wasn't just a businessman, was he?'

'I beg your pardon?'

'Well, everybody has friends, don't they?'

'Oh. Yes, I see what you mean.' Dennis ran a hand through his hair. 'Yes. Peter had a lot of decent friends.'

'Like you?'

Dennis was beginning to get unnerved. 'Yeah,' he said, a trifle defensively, 'including me.'

'You were good friends?'

'Yeah. Peter was a good mate. It was him talked me into staying here.'

The accent, thought Fitz, is beginning to slip. 'From?' he asked.

'Essex. Romford.'

Ah. Hence the accent. The one underneath. 'So Philby Medical originally operated in the UK?'

'Yes.' Dennis was beginning to regret the reference to the move. The move that had happened as a result of an accidental meeting with Peter Yang. Peter had said that Hong Kong was a land of opportunity: a frontier town for people like Dennis. A place where huge amounts of money could be made. He had been extremely surprised when Dennis had taken him at his word and arrived, with a one-way ticket, ten years previously. Dennis hadn't looked the type.

Janet unwittingly saved him from divulging more. 'The day before the murder,' she said as she handed the buff file to Wise, 'Peter Yang wrote you a cheque.'

'Yes. For an order. He did every quarter. It's being processed at the moment, actually.'

Actually. Fitz clocked the change of register. The accent had gone.

'It's all paid for,' continued Dennis. Like Carter before him, he suddenly looked sad. 'I assume that Nancy – his wife – is going to take over the business. Poor woman.'

'You'll be at the funeral, then?'

''Course.' Dennis didn't quite meet Fitz's eye. 'It's too early to talk business, but I've told Nancy I'll help where I can.'

Definitely not social, remembered Fitz. So what's all this 'helping Nancy' business? Why assume friendship where it hadn't existed? And then he remembered where he was. He imagined the vultures gathering over Peter Yang's grave; the 'friends' clamouring round the grieving widow, eager to help, desperate to get a slice of the action. Yes, Dennis was smarmy. But there was something else. Something, he suspected, to do with a past in Romford, Essex.

'How come the cheque was for three times the regular order?' Wise, taking his colleagues by surprise, had located the recent transaction – and its predecessors – in the file.

Dennis, however, had already thought of the answer to that one. He shrugged, only half-interested. 'Peter had made some new contacts on the mainland. In case you hadn't noticed,' he added with a smile, 'the Chinese are getting very Chinese this year. But Peter', he added hurriedly, 'was keen for us to keep working things out.'

Working things out, thought Fitz. An odd phrase to use. Unless, of course, things *hadn't* been working out. He leaned forward, blatantly antagonistic. 'You find the money sexy, Dennis?'

Dennis didn't know what to say; how to react. Of *course* he found money sexy. This was Hong Kong. He looked at Fitz through narrowed eyes. 'Odd question,' was all he said.

Wise, once more scrutinizing the file, suddenly flashed a smile at Dennis. 'He's an odd bloke.'

Fitz was furious. The moment had been lightened; Philby was smiling. He wanted him back on the defensive. 'Here from Essex?' he said with a sneer. 'From the arsehole of nowhere to a major world centre. Everyone talking dollars, talking millions.'

Dennis shrugged again. ''S like anywhere else. The

money's relative.'

But Fitz was relentless.

'Well-travelled?' he demanded.

'Me? Not particularly. Why?'

'You know anybody with a grudge against him?' Wise, suddenly, was hammering away like Fitz.

But Dennis just laughed. 'No.'

'We think', said Janet, 'that Peter Yang knew his killer.'

'Really?'

'When did you last see him?' Janet, too, raised a polite eyebrow.

Dennis laughed again. This time incredulously. 'You mean I'm a *suspect*?'

'Formality,' said Janet.

How much, thought Philby, do they *know*? 'Peter came here on Tuesday. Didn't stay long.'

'Witnesses?'

Dennis shrugged. 'Everybody in the building.'

Fitz leaned forward, a question forming on his lips. Janet robbed him of the opportunity of asking it. Standing up, she nodded and smiled at Dennis.

'Thank you', she said, 'for your time.' Wise stood up with her, as did Dennis. Fitz remained seated for a moment. He was annoyed at Janet over her high-handed manner, her less than subtle demonstration that she was boss: he was annoyed at her for not being Panhandle. Panhandle would have noticed Philby's momentary hesitation, the flicker of fear that had registered in his deep blue eyes.

Dennis turned to Fitz. He was confident now, certain that he had passed this interrogation with flying colours. His half-smile conveyed mild irritation; annoyance at Fitz for taking up too much of his precious time. Dennis Philby, important businessman, had better things to do and better people to see.

With a broad grin that rather disconcerted Dennis, Fitz suddenly accepted the silent invitation. As he followed Janet and Wise out of the room, he was still debating with himself whether there was more or less to Dennis Philby than met the eye.

Dennis sat motionless at his desk after they had left. The panic had been silly. He should have known the police would come: of *course* they would come. In a strange way, he had actually *wanted* them to come, to interrogate him, to play cat-and-mouse together. And he had won the game. He felt elated. And to his surprise, he also felt disappointed. What now? He didn't want to play any more games. He wanted his Su-Lin.

The thought of his girlfriend brought the shadows back into Dennis's eyes. The haunted look was back; the controlled businessman collapsed again. Su-Lin. If the police investigated him further, they would find out about her. They would find out that she had been his constant companion for five years. What else would they find? That people were silly, prejudiced; that they considered Su-Lin, not himself, to be the brains behind the business? That she was calm and cool and collected and he was volatile? Dennis knew all the rumours. That was why he had distanced himself from people, from 'friends'. Nobody, in any case, had friends in Hong Kong. They were too intent on getting what they wanted: money and power.

Dennis grinned. Money and power. He had both now. How easy it had been, after taking Su-Lin to the shipping crate that night, to go to Peter Yang's office; to plead a change of heart and to apologize for his earlier bad behaviour. He had been overwrought, he explained to Peter. Stressed. Selling the business was anyway what he had planned to do. He would accept a cheque right now. And Peter had written the cheque. How trusting. And how agile Dennis had been to reach for the Jockey Club trophy – a real inspiration, that one. Peter hadn't died immediately, but he hadn't been in pain. Not really. He had been too busy watching Dennis. He had looked on in awe, listened to Dennis's quiet words, his assumption of power. He had died, Dennis seemed to remember, as his hands were being tied. Fitting, that. Died as he had prayed to Dennis.

Su-Lin, Dennis suddenly remembered. He was supposed to be thinking about Su-Lin. She had disappeared, hadn't she? Walked out on him; taken her suitcases. Maybe she had gone to her parents. Wretched people. Why did they all have to have families? Why did they all run back to mummy and daddy? Didn't they ever *grow up*? He had grown up, hadn't he? And quickly. His eyes narrowed. Oh yes, childhood had been such a riot he'd abandoned it as soon as he had been able. And they'd been relieved. Both of them. He'd become an embarrassment – a horrible reminder.

Then Dennis's face softened as he thought about his baby. Nothing and no one was going to jeopardize that – his great achievement. Su-Lin had tried and failed. She would not be able to try again.

Then he remembered Su-Lin's parents. She hadn't gone to them, gone crying back to the family nest. They would already be worried about her. Wei Wei, who had ironically stopped making 'wedding' and 'baby' noises. Al, with his strange, sidelong glances towards Dennis: his unvoiced but obvious opinion that Su-Lin shouldn't be going out with a *gweilo*, that Dennis wasn't good enough for her. Ha! He would show them. But first he must tell them she had disappeared. He must be cunning. He must get there before the police.

'Where is she?' Dennis stormed into the mini-market. He didn't have to pretend to be agitated; to appear at the end of his tether. The drive to Shau Kei Wan had been appalling. Traffic everywhere. *People* all around. Didn't they know he was in a hurry?

'Where is she?' he boomed again, ignoring the smiling Mei Ming at the counter as he bounded up the cramped staircase and into the apartment. Wei Wei was in the main room, ironing. So was Al, watching TV. They looked up, startled, as Dennis's angry presence filled the room. 'Please, Wei Wei,' he begged. 'Where is she?'

Wei Wei just stared. Dennis looked as if he had gone mad. He appeared suddenly gaunt, new lines had appeared at the corners of his mouth and round his eyes.

Those beautiful eyes. Not beautiful now.

His panic transferred itself to Wei Wei. 'What are you saying?' she stammered, suddenly terrified. 'Why you ask me where she is?'

Dennis fixed her with an accusatory look. 'She *told* you she was gonna leave me, didn't she?' Suddenly he hated Wei Wei.

'Huh?' Precise even in her alarm, Wei Wei switched off the iron and placed it upright on the board. But her hand was shaking.

Dennis came closer. 'Leave me,' he barked. '*Left* me. She's gone. Suitcases,' he said, angrily waving his arms around, alarming Wei Wei even further. 'I want to know where she is.'

Real terror flickered in Wei Wei's eyes. Turning to her husband, she translated for him in gunfire Cantonese. He, for so long the passive observer of the life that went on around him, leaped to his feet. The owlish eyes, accentuated by the round glasses, bored straight into Dennis's. He knew his daughter, his sensible, clever eldest daughter. He knew that she and Dennis had had their ups and downs. He knew – or at least he suspected – that things hadn't been going too well of late. But above all else, he knew that Su-Lin would never, *ever* disappear without telling anyone. Unless, of course, she had no option.

Dennis's rage cooled into an icy fury as he looked at the elder Tangs. He could read the suspicion in Al's face; the accusation in Wei Wei's. So it was his fault, was it? His fault that their daughter no longer chose to share everything with them? He sneered down at the elderly couple. 'Oh,' he said, dripping sarcasm. 'I can see how upset you are for *me*.' He came even closer to Wei Wei; close enough for her to see the beads of sweat breaking out on his forehead, to smell the rancid, gastric breath, to see that he was trembling all over with some pent-up emotion. Wei Wei stepped back.

Suddenly Dennis looked lost. 'You don't know', he asked in a plaintive, little-boy's voice, 'where she's gone?'

'No.'

Dennis looked from one to the other; from Wei Wei's anxious face to Al's suspicious one. Then, without another word, he turned and left the apartment. Wei Wei ran after him.

'You think she's safe?' she shouted as he ran down the stairs.

Dennis's face, mocking now, hard and adult, looked back up at her. 'How the hell should I know?' he sneered. 'You're the one she tells her secrets to.' Then, again ignoring Mei Ming, he ran back through the supermarket and out into the street towards his car.

By the time he reached it, his mood had changed again. He was pleased with himself; he had acted the part to perfection; had made a convincing show of being at once angry and upset, lost and suspicious, beside himself with worry. Driven almost to the end of his tether. He hadn't, he realized with no little surprise, even had to *act* that much. It had all seemed to come so naturally. Then he gunned the engine and turned the car in the direction of the tunnel. Su-Lin would be missing him, she would be lonely. Adjusting to new circumstances, he knew, took time. Then, suddenly, he laughed out loud. What had he said the other day? That he would never move to the mainland; to a poky hovel in Mongkok? The idea hadn't seemed to bother Su-Lin, she was used to small spaces, confined living quarters. Perhaps she was enjoying the shipping crate after all.

Su-Lin was curled up on the floor when he entered the crate. He smiled when he saw her: wasn't that what they called the foetal position? Stepping closer, he noticed the book that must have dropped from her hands as contented sleep overcame her. He picked it up. It was, of course, one of the books he had bought her. *Pregnancy and Childbirth*. Such a matter-of-fact title for such a momentous concept. Dennis smiled again and stood still, revelling in the sight of the pregnant woman at his feet. He felt almost tearful, overcome with joy.

Su-Lin looked up at him from under her lashes. She couldn't, in the dim light of her lamp and Dennis's torch, read his expression. Was he angry? Sad? Filled with remorse? Or was he happy to be back with his girlfriend and unborn child in their new, secure home? She suspected the latter: she had suspected it the moment she had heard the approaching footsteps. That was why she had grabbed the wretched book. It had fallen open at a page that mocked her, at a chapter entitled 'Your Partner's Reaction to Pregnancy'. She had been unable to stop herself from reading for a moment, from gleaning, with horrified fascination, advice on how to cope with your lover's jealousy – or his stifling over-protectiveness. The stillness, the curled-up position she had assumed when Dennis had opened the door of the crate had not been faked. The words on the page had caused her to go numb, to draw her knees up to her abdomen and close her eyes in the feeble hope that the world would go away. And if she closed her eyes, if she was unable to see anything, then perhaps nothing and nobody would see her.

Dennis's determined approach told her that her hopes were futile. As he picked up the book and stood looking down at her, Su-Lin sought desperately to recapture her earlier resolution, to remember the plan she had conceived during the long, appallingly hot day. Even as she did so, she felt a tremor of revulsion. She must be calm, pleased to see Dennis. She must appear to be happy – and she had to play for time. She had conceived a particularly macabre ploy to achieve the latter.

She steeled herself not to flinch when Dennis bent down to kiss her. Instead she moaned slightly; an indication of an impending, pleasurable return to consciousness.

Dennis kissed her again and ruffled her hair. ''S only me, sleepyhead. It's okay.' His voice was tender and loving. He would, she knew, be smiling when she opened her eyes.

He was. Su-Lin fluttered her lashes, opened her eyes, blinked and smiled a lazy, happy smile. Then she yawned and stretched luxuriantly. *Act*, she told herself as she looked at Dennis. Quell the desire to lash out at him, to scream, to heed the queasiness in her stomach and throw up all over her collection of vitamin pills and mother-and-child books.

She reached up and touched Dennis's cheek. 'I was just dreaming about you.'

'Me?' Dennis looked delighted. 'Dreaming what?'

Su-Lin sat up and looked coyly at Dennis from behind the hair that cascaded over her face. 'You'd laugh,' she said.

'No, I wouldn't,' replied Dennis, already laughing, excited by the demure yet teasing expression.

'I dreamed', said Su-Lin, looking up, 'that we'd just got married.' She hoped the smile reached her eyes, prayed that they betrayed no sign of calculation.

Dennis's only reaction was to stop smiling and to look at her with an even greater, more intense passion.

'It was a hot day,' she continued. 'You couldn't see my feet because the dress came all the way down to my shoes.' She gestured to her bare and shackled feet. Dennis's eyes followed her hands, but she couldn't tell if the new, broader smile was directed at the manacles round her wrist or if it was born of the idea of marriage. Both sickened her. 'You couldn't see my face,' she added, now running her hands from her face to her chest, 'because the veil came all the way down to here. And then, when you lifted it to kiss me, everything felt . . . perfect.' She ignored the lurch in her gut and smiled at Dennis.

He stared back, nonplussed, completely perplexed by her revelation. His head spun; he couldn't fix on his own emotions. Then, stunned disbelief shining from his eyes, he leaned towards her. 'You mean . . . are you asking me to marry you?'

Su-Lin didn't reply. Instead, as if still recounting her dream, she looked past him and into the shadows of her prison. 'I fell asleep,' she lied, 'thinking about the first time I ever met you . . . handsome for an Englishman, polite for a businessman.' Then she turned back to him. 'You said I was the most beautiful woman you'd ever met.'

The words had the desired effect. It was now Dennis who looked bashful, slightly embarrassed; pleased but coy. 'Are you asking me', he repeated, 'to marry you?' The question was uttered in tones of wonder – yet the undertones were unmistakable. Dennis was thrilled.

Su-Lin shook her head. 'I'm waiting for you to ask me.'

'Eh?' Doubt flickered in Dennis's eyes. 'What're you talking about?' Then he remembered: he looked down at Su-Lin's stomach and smiled again. 'You're thinking about the baby?'

'Just ask me.' Teasing again, Su-Lin let her hair fall forward. Not the baby, she thought. Keep him away from that subject.

'I've asked you a dozen times.' Dennis sounded peeved. 'You don't want a wedding.'

Suspicious, thought Su-Lin. A flicker of suspicion. She shot him her most dazzling smile. 'Your timing was bad.' Then she leaned towards him. She ran her tongue over her lips, inviting him, seducing him with suggestion. 'Ask me now,' she purred.

At that moment she forgot her shackles, forgot that she was this man's prisoner, helpless in the face of his every crazy whim. All she could think about was the sudden sense of power that surged through her. Was this, she wondered, what it was like to be mad? It sickened her — but it also excited her. Control; gaining the upper hand. She felt she had it at that moment.

Dennis too was excited. He could feel Su-Lin's breath on his face, could see the sparkle in her eyes, the moistness on her lips. He felt giddy. 'You'd have to come to England with me,' he suddenly said. 'We'd have to get out of here. Away', he added in a high, agitated voice, 'from all this mess.'

'I know.' Su-Lin touched his lips with a gentle finger. 'Sssh. Ask me, Dennis. Ask me.' Now all she felt was an unbearable tension. She had sown the seeds of something new in Dennis's warped mind, and they were taking root.

Dennis squared his shoulders and looked her in the eye. 'Su-Lin, I want you to marry me.' His sudden pomposity, the gravitas with which he made his proposal, was almost comical. In any other circumstances Su-Lin would have teased him about it; but not now, not in this dark, fetid shipping crate in which she was trapped. Remembering her shackles, she fought back a new wave of nausea. Her resistance to marriage had been fierce, still was. She had never forgotten her mother's tales of her Chinese ancestors; of the grandmother who had been beaten by her husband; of the great-grandmother

143

who had been close to the Empress Dowager and the Manchu court. Su-Lin's current proximity to Dennis echoed in horrific parallel that lady's situation: she had had no choice but to remain close to the court. She had lived in permanent agony, her feet bound into tiny shoes, rendering her immobile. She had lived and died according to the customs of men: never having the chance to escape her husband nor the environment he had chosen for her. Tears sprang to Su-Lin's eyes.

Dennis thought they were tears of joy. 'Su-Lin,' he repeated. 'I want you to marry me.'

'Two conditions.' The words came too suddenly, were too abrupt. Su-Lin couldn't help it; she was looking at the shackles binding her feet, envisaging the unending horror of imprisonment.

Her response, she saw, had startled Dennis. She leaned forward and, with a broad smile, softened the blow. 'You promise me, on your life, I get the best wedding Hong Kong's ever seen.'

Dennis greeted that one with a manic laugh. Then, puppet-like, he began to nod; his head went up and down in an exaggerated, unnatural fashion as tears of joy flowed down his cheeks.

'And you promise me,' continued Su-Lin, 'in England, when we start again, you talk to me. When you look at me, you see someone you can trust, someone who loves you.' She looked up and met his gaze. 'We look after each other, okay?'

'Yes!' Dennis threw his arms round her and hugged her close. Then he released her and, more gently, took her face between his hands. 'Yes!' he whispered, his mind filled with visions of the extravagant, beautiful wedding ceremony they would have. Not only would it be the best wedding Hong Kong had ever seen, it would also be the most moving. Smiling, he leaned forward and kissed his bride-to-be.

Su-Lin laughed, a veil of ecstasy covering her agony. Had it worked? Had she really got through to him? Had she delved beyond the madness to reach a core of sanity? She didn't care how long it lasted; all she wanted was his trust. Even if it was fleeting, even if it only lasted a few minutes more, that would be enough. Still laughing, she pulled away from him. Looking into his eyes, she willed him to accept that it was all over now, that there would be no recrimination, only forgiveness and then everlasting joy. 'Let's go home,' she whispered.

Dennis nodded and stood up. 'Yes,' he said. Proud and adoring, he looked down at her, at his precious, delicate Su-Lin. He could hardly believe that she had agreed to be his for ever. Then he turned and walked towards the entrance of the crate.

Su-Lin watched, horrified, as he went. 'Where're you going?' she stammered, unable to disguise her panic. 'Take me with you!'

Dennis turned round – but not back. 'Not yet,' he said, still smiling. 'I'm in charge of this one. I want this to be a surprise.'

'Dennis!' Su-Lin's voice was a desperate, piercing scream. 'Dennis . . .!'

But her anguished cries fell on deaf ears. The door

slammed, a deafening crunch of metal against metal, and Su-Lin was once again in darkness and alone.

Janet was aware that she had ended the interview with Dennis Philby too abruptly for Fitz's liking. And she knew she had ended it for reasons that were rather less than professional. She had found Fitz's sudden aggression distasteful, had objected to the way he had suddenly pounced on Philby. And the questions about Romford, Essex had been both rude and irrelevant. Hours after they had left the premises of Philby Medical she was still wondering why English people were so obsessed about where they came from, about what class they belonged to. Fitz, she decided, obviously had a chip on his shoulder. He was probably a poor boy made good – no wonder he resented Dennis Philby. The younger man had obviously done a lot better. And, she reflected as she typed up her notes, he was a great deal better-looking. Janet had rather warmed to Dennis Philby.

Yet she had retained enough objectivity to decide that Philby should remain a suspect. An unlikely one, maybe, but a suspect nonetheless. Rather than gaining from Peter Yang's death, he was surely likely to lose business because of it.

What had Fitz said about the murderer, she wondered as she tapped at her keyboard. An underachiever? Philby didn't appear to fit that bill either. He looked smart; rich. A silver BMW had been parked outside his office. No doubt he was one of those Brits who relished the expat lifestyle; who spent fortunes on eating out every night and on flying abroad for the weekend. And no doubt he lived in Happy Valley or Mid-Levels. Maybe he was even a neighbour of hers. She grinned at the thought. Dennis Philby, she knew, would be appalled at the very idea. Rich *gweilos* and Hong Kong Chinese policewomen living in close proximity: not something he would relish. Then Janet sighed and leaned forward to her computer again. She supposed, if Dennis Philby were to remain on the suspect list, she really ought to find out his home address. With a grim smile, she typed an instruction to herself on the document on her screen. The grim smile was in anticipation of Fitz's trying to read the document – a task he would find impossible since it was written in Cantonese.

Finishing her task, she looked at her watch and grimaced. Nine o'clock. She rarely worked this late on a 'normal' day. Yet normality, after the murders of Peter Yang and Dr Sunny, was a thing of the past. And her routine had been further fractured by the presence of Wise and Fitz on the case – and by Ellison's insistence that their help would be invaluable. As far as Janet was concerned, they had thus far done nothing apart from irritate her. And, if she were honest, intimidate her. Earlier in the day, she had begun to warm to them. That warmth had disappeared after the Dennis Philby episode. If Fitz wanted to continue with his macho posturing, then that was fine by her. She was eminently capable of giving as good as she got.

She leaned back in her chair and surveyed the room. Was their world like this? Was it better equipped; the staff more efficient? Was that why Fitz was so damned superior all the time? She doubted, if British police dramas were anything to go by, that the Manchester station would be anything like as clean, well-appointed and spacious as the Hong Kong headquarters. Maybe that, perversely, was grounds for the superiority: if they could solve the gruesome, violent crimes of which Fitz had spoken with few resources and not enough staff, then why couldn't Hong Kong do the same? Janet sighed and leaned back towards her computer – and away from the only object in the room that definitively set it apart from its British or even American counterparts – the huge red and gold shrine in the far corner. Janet took it completely for granted: western visitors – Fitz included – always did a double-take when they noticed it. The size of a large wardrobe, it sat incongruously between two filing cabinets, yet jutted out far enough to get in everyone's way. It was further identifiable by its smell: the sweet aroma of incense that wafted up to the twisted face of the god on its fascia. Few people were bothered by the sharp, pungent smell: it was overpowered, night and day, by a smell common to police stations the world over – cigarette smoke. All day long, cigarettes were lit and extinguished as the officers went about their business. But now, at this late hour, only Benny Ho, silently working at the desk opposite her own, was smoking.

It was Benny who saw the new arrival first. Clad in his customary white coat and, as usual, wrinkling his nose in disgust at the smell of Benny's cigarettes, he marched swiftly up to Janet. He, the pathologist, was none too pleased about working so late. The only compensation was that he had spent the last few hours on the autopsy of Dr Sunny – an activity that had produced some fairly startling results. He was carrying those results, Benny noticed, as he approached Janet. Without a word, and with only a slight nod to Benny, he dropped the photographs on Janet's desk. Startled, and none too pleased herself at the stealthy interruption, she swung round to protest; but the pathologist, now smiling, was already walking away. The results spoke for themselves.

Annoyed, Janet snatched at the photos and pulled her anglepoise closer. Typical, she thought. The wretched man was really getting a buzz out of the Yang and Sunny murders. A buzz that was verging on the distinctly theatrical.

Then, as she studied the first photograph, Janet too became histrionic. She let out an involuntary little scream; her eyes widened in horror; she looked, non-plussed, over the desk at Benny and then back at the macabre picture in front of her. Alarmed, Benny was beside her in a flash. And then he too moaned in disgusted, horrified disbelief. The photograph was a mortuary close-up of Dr Sunny's face. The mouth, closed and inoffensive when the body had been found, was now agape, held open by a brutal-looking medical clamp. Both Janet had Benny had seen similar shots; undignified, maybe, but hardly shocking. What shocked them were the contents of the mouth. Whoever had killed Dr Sunny had not murdered him for the money he had been carrying: his motive had not been gain. Something more sinister; something more studied had made the killer take the money – and then ram it into the doctor's mouth. And now, in the photograph, the mouth was yawning open and the money spilling out. It made for a horrible sight; and a horrible realization. It was as if the murderer was looking at Janet through his victim's dead eyes, mocking her; teasing her; knowing that she had jumped to the wrong conclusion about his motive.

But if it wasn't money, thought Janet, what on earth was it?

Janet didn't trust herself to look at Benny again. He would be able to read the despair in her eyes, the near-defeat. He would realize that she was now out of her depth. He would know – perhaps he knew already – that she had very little option but to go crawling back to Fitz and admit that she was firmly back at square one.

Fitz had spent a large part of the evening wondering what on earth he was doing. Had he been seduced by two thousand dollars a day and the Ritz Carlton Hotel? Greater men, he supposed, had capitulated for less – but was he actually doing his reputation any good? He was well aware that Ellison's primary motivation for inviting him to join the investigation was to bask in the vicarious glory of its success. But then Ellison was a prat. Janet Lee Cheung was a much tougher proposition and, he felt, a much more professional operator. Yet her pride was getting in the way of their task. She had made no bones about her objections to Fitz. Fitz could live with that; he was used to being disliked. What he found insupportable was Janet's brusque, dismissive attitude towards his craft and her dogged determination to hang on to the reins – both being nothing more than covers for her insecurity. Janet, he knew, was out of her depth. He also knew that something, at some point, would trigger an admission of that fact.

He didn't expect the trigger to be pulled so soon. Unaware of what had just happened at the police station, he was contemplating another nightcap when he heard the sharp knock on the door. He looked, frowning, at his watch. Eleven o'clock. Who the hell came knocking at that hour? The bell-hop, probably. Fitz had palmed him off with a miniature of vodka from the minibar instead of a tip after he had carried his baggage up to the room. The young porter had been seeking revenge ever since, appearing at the door on all manner of trumped-up, irritating errands. Fitz marched towards the door, intent on sending the man away with a large flea in his ear.

But the person standing on the threshold had no intention of being sent away. The moment Fitz threw open the door, Janet Lee Cheung stormed in.

'Hey!' Completely wrong-footed, Fitz turned to her in astonishment. 'What time do you call this? What time do you work till?' He was on the point of making another, ruder remark when Janet turned round to face him. There was no trace of any earlier arrogance, no supercilious curl of the lip. All he could read on her face was distress.

'This', she said in a strained voice, 'is not what I'm

151

used to. It's not what I'm used to.'

Suddenly concerned, immediately attuned to her near-desperation, Fitz walked calmly up to her. 'What's happened, Janet?' Janet was too keyed-up to notice that he had just used her Christian name for the first time.

'This,' she said, handing him the envelope. 'You were right about Dr Sunny,' she added as she watched him open it. 'He wasn't robbed. We found the money.'

'Jesus!' Fitz was looking at the photographs, at the grotesquely distorted mouth. At the money.

Janet took a deep breath. 'Please don't look at those and tell me you get used to it.'

Fitz looked up at her. No, he thought, seeing the trembling lip. I won't tell you that. And anyway, I'd be lying. You never get used to it. You never get used to the surprises slung at you by the rest of the human race.

As if on cue, Charlie Wise barged in from the adjoining room. 'Aye, aye!' he said, beaming at Janet. 'I thought I heard you.'

Janet smiled back. The moment had passed. With his loud Geordie accent and cheery manner, Wise had unwittingly lifted the atmosphere. He looked from her to Fitz. 'Anybody hungry? I could eat a bloody horse!'

After seeing the photographs, food was the last thing on Janet's mind. Yet, surprisingly, she found that she was hungry. 'Yes,' she said. 'Fitz?'

Fitz shrugged. He hadn't eaten either; the price of the drinks he had consumed in the hotel bar had seen to that. 'Okay. Why not?'

'My treat,' said Janet. 'But not', she added with a

sudden grin, 'in the hotel. I know just the place for a late-night snack.'

Relieved, Wise smiled again. In Fuengirola, the meals had been included in the package. Here he had to fend for himself. Going hungry was a preferable alternative to the precarious business of ordering meals in a foreign country. Especially one where they used chopsticks.

Janet took them to a noodle bar in an alley off Chater Road. Her confidence, she realized as she led the way, was returning. And it was thanks to Fitz. Their brief exchange of looks in his hotel bedroom; his instinctive understanding of her panic; her own tacit admission that she needed help had put them back on course again. More importantly, she sensed that they had established new ground rules. She was still in charge of the case, but now she was prepared to listen to Fitz's opinions. And to accept them.

But assuming control came naturally to her. She led her companions into the brightly lit restaurant, weaved her way through the throng and, with an authoritative bark at a passing waiter, commandeered a table. Fitz and Wise were happy to follow her lead: neither man would have had the confidence even to set foot in the place. They were the only westerners in the restaurant.

'Shall I order?' said Janet as they sat down.

'Aye.' Wise peered at the indecipherable hieroglyphs on the menu. 'As long as you don't order rat.'

Janet suppressed a grin.

'And as long', added an adamant Fitz, 'as you order wine. Two bottles.'

'Sure? You'd be better off with beer in here.'

'No. Wine.'

Janet shrugged. The wine – if indeed there was any – would be filthy. But then if the waistlines of both her companions were anything to go by, quantity, not quality, was their standard of judgement.

Fitz showed the photographs to Wise as Janet grabbed a passing waiter and shouted their order.

'Bloody hell!' Even to a senior detective, hardened by years of witnessing the seamier side of life, the images came as something of a shock. He raised an eyebrow and turned to Fitz. 'Dr Sunny?'

'The same.'

'And so', he said, catching Janet's eye, 'he was killed by the same man?'

Janet nodded.

A glint came into Fitz's eye as the wine appeared. With it came a sudden garrulousness. 'With a guy like this,' he said as he began to pour, 'you've no guarantees. Except that he hates himself, hates what he's doing. Enough to want to be stopped.'

Janet looked dubious. 'But if he wants to be caught, why's he hiding?'

Fitz wagged a finger. 'Not caught – stopped. You're leading the investigation, he knows you're in charge. He's never met you but he's making you responsible for his crimes.'

About to object, Janet was interrupted by the waiter arriving with a tray of food. Wise, who had been surreptitiously trying to master his chopsticks under the table, perked up when he noticed the little spoons accompanying the various courses. He deposited his chopsticks firmly and with relief on the empty place beside him.

Janet, too, was having problems with the food. She stared at the three little bowls of soup that she had ordered along with the rice, fish, meat and vegetable dishes. She had ordered the soup, a speciality of the season, without thinking. What on earth would her guests make of it, she wondered?

She needn't have worried. Wise was already attacking it with the same gusto as Fitz was demolishing the wine. 'Lovely chicken broth, this,' he said. 'Almost as good as Reenie's.'

Janet lifted her bowl to her mouth to hide her smile. Crisis over. No need to tell him that the meat in the soup was actually snake.

Fitz's mind, however, was still on the case. 'If all you do is think like Pavlov's dog,' he said as he refilled his glass, 'then you've no chance. Think like your man; think like you're desperate . . .'

'When he gets to this stage in Manchester,' said Wise, noting Janet's bemused expression, 'we chuck a bucket of cold water over him.'

Fitz pretended he hadn't heard. 'You've got to acknowledge this man's *pain*,' he advised.

Janet made a moue of distaste. 'I can't do that. Dr Sunny left three children aged . . .'

'That's not your problem.'

'. . . three, five and seven.'

Fitz shrugged and reached for the duck. 'Not your concern.'

Janet sighed. He was right. The three fatherless children were irrelevant; extraneous details in a murder hunt. They had no place in her investigation; an investigation that wasn't going anywhere very fast. 'I still', she said with emphasis, 'don't buy the motive. A wealthy exporter and an obstetrician. If we can't connect them, then we can't . . .'

'An obstetrician?' Fitz dropped his chopsticks and rounded on her. 'Dr Sunny was an obstetrician?'

'Yes.' Janet rolled her eyes. For a psychologist this man was showing extremely limited powers of observation. 'You were with me when I viewed his office.' A touch of her old condescension was back in her voice. 'It's on the door,' she finished with a pitying smile.

'Not in English it's not.'

'Oh.' Janet shrugged and lowered her eyes; an elegant, unspoken apology.

Fitz's mind was now racing. 'Some babies survive,' he said to no one in particular. 'Some babies don't get that far.'

'Miscarriage?' This from Wise.

'Abortion?' said Janet, cursing herself for not thinking earlier about the implications of the doctor's speciality.

Fitz turned to her. 'What's an abortion cost on the island these days?'

'Six thousand dollars.'

Both men were taken aback by the promptness of Janet's response. Janet noted their reaction and flushed.

'Six and a half,' she corrected, reaching for a garlic prawn. 'Maybe.'

Interesting, thought Fitz. Very interesting. Then he forced his mind back to the reason for this conversation. 'Okay, she's pregnant. He wants the kid – she doesn't. So she arranges the abortion in secret. He finds out and murders the doctor.'

'I still don't understand', said Janet, 'what Peter Yang's murder has to do with this.'

Fitz waved a chopstick in the air. 'Glittering example of success. Yang has everything this guy doesn't.' Then, his mind still focused on the photographs, he pointed to the envelope on the table beside Janet. 'The killer's wife's planning to abort a baby they both know they can't afford. Otherwise, why ram that amount – that precise amount – down your doctor's throat?'

'Why not stick it in the bank if you're that skint?'

Fitz glared at his colleague. 'Because, Charlie, the principle means more than the money.'

Janet nodded. 'Yes. It hangs together.'

But Wise was now the sceptical one. 'Oh aye,' he said. 'Just like a wrestler's nuts.'

Janet grinned and then turned to Fitz. 'So: the wife. We can assume her appointment for the termination was going to be soon; that the killer had no time to waste in murdering Sunny.'

'Er . . . yes.' Fitz wasn't sure whether it was a statement or a question. Something in Janet's eyes told him it was the former; she had already demonstrated her familiarity with the process of abortion.

'So,' continued Janet, 'unless the wife is illiterate – which, given that she was being treated by the expensive Dr Sunny, I doubt – then she's going to have read about his death. What does she do now?'

'And what', added Wise, 'does the husband do?'

Dennis had known exactly where to go. You could buy everything at Temple Street Market. It stayed open till late at night, the vendors purveying all manner of goods – legal and illegal – to residents and tourists alike. And the goods he had in mind were anything but illegal. Apart, of course, from the document. But that was only a minor detail, and he might not even be able to find it here. As long as he located one within the next few days, he would be fine. Su-Lin really had come up trumps. Marriage was definitely the answer. Everything had now fallen into place.

The apartment in Happy Valley, however, was his first stop after leaving the cargo basin. Some of what he already needed was there, barely used, hanging in the back of his wardrobe. He grinned when he found the weighty bag he was looking for. Then, slinging it over his shoulder, he hurried out of the bedroom and through the apartment. Temple Street, back on the Kowloon side, was waiting.

Dennis was back with Su-Lin at the same time as Janet Lee Cheung and her British colleagues walked into the noodle bar in Central. By the time they had settled down to their snake soup, their prawns, their duck and their wine, he had helped Su-Lin into the outfit he had bought at Temple Street. He didn't appear to notice that horrified disbelief had reduced her to a near-catatonic state. Nor did he realize that the tears coursing down her cheeks were not, like his own, tears of joy.

When Charlie Wise asked the question about what the killer was doing, Dennis was asking his own question. He found it difficult to find the words, even more difficult to articulate them. Su-Lin looked so beautiful, so fragile. And she was, like him, humbled by the occasion.

'Su-Lin Tang,' he stammered as he held her hand. 'Do you take this man, Dennis Colin Philby, as your lawful wedded husband, to have and to hold from this day forward as long as you both shall live?'

Su-Lin didn't reply immediately. Dennis didn't blame her; she was savouring them, the most precious words she would ever hear in her life. Her head was bowed, her face hidden by the veil. Of that, at least, Su-Lin was glad. Yet she was still numb with disbelief. When Dennis had returned, she had assumed the parcels had been more supplies. It had never entered her mind that the large bag would contain his morning-suit. And never in a million years, not even in the depths of her worst nightmares, could she have imagined what was in the box.

And now she was wearing it: the snow-white wedding dress that cascaded down to her feet – feet now clad in too-tight white shoes, and still bound by her chains. Su-Lin bit back a sob. The terrible travesty of a wedding was actually happening. She would have to reply. 'I do,' she whispered as the bile rose in her throat.

'Do you,' gulped Dennis, 'Dennis Colin Philby, take this woman, Su-Lin Tang, to have and to hold, to love and to cherish and to . . . to love her . . . protect her as long as you both shall live?' Dennis was so choked with emotion that he could hardly speak. Fighting to hold back the tears, he answered his own question. 'I do.'

Then he took a ring from his pocket and took Su-Lin's hand in his own. 'You may now', he intoned as he forced a ring on her swollen finger, 'kiss the bride.'

Su-Lin had no choice but to look up. In a way, it was better now. She had exhausted her reserves of disbelief, of horror and disgust. She was so drained there was nothing left: no hatred, no shock, no desperation. Just total emptiness.

'This', whispered Dennis as his lips puckered towards her own, 'is the happiest day of my life.'

Chapter Six

'Is it normal to have that many in one week?'

'That many what?'

'Terminations.'

Janet stared fixedly at the road ahead. 'In November, yes.'

'Oh.' Seeing the sudden whiteness of Janet's knuckles on the steering-wheel, Fitz dropped the subject. He was professional enough to know that he was venturing onto forbidden territory; human enough to want to go further. Janet would tell him in her own good time. Then again, she might not. She wasn't, after all, his patient.

The word made Fitz look down at the list of names in his lap; the list of Dr Sunny's patients from the day of his murder onwards. Sunny's receptionist, still shell-shocked, had been reluctant to open his files to the police. 'Confidential,' she had wailed to Janet when they had called at his consulting-rooms first thing in the morning. 'Essential,' Janet had replied. 'Don't you want to find out who killed your boss?' The receptionist, clearly opposite in nature to her late boss's name, had shot Janet a mutinous look and, muttering darkly, proceeded to open the filing cabinets.

Both Wise and Fitz had been staggered by the twenty abortions booked in for the week following Sunny's murder. Termination, it seemed, was a synonym for contraception in the island. Yet they knew, after last night's conversation, that Dr Sunny's patients were the only leads they had. One of them, surely, would be the killer's wife or girlfriend. The only problem lay in the unanswered questions of the previous night. *What did the girlfriend do now? What did the killer do now?* That both would disappear for ever – the former to meet her death – was the answer that remained unvoiced.

But at least, thought Fitz, they had some names. The first was for a patient, one Catherine Wilson, whom Sunny had seen on the day of his murder. Had she seen something or somebody unexpected in the surgery? Would her boyfriend be the killer? Fitz doubted it; whoever Catherine Wilson's boyfriend was, it was a safe bet that he would have encouraged the abortion. Catherine Wilson, according to Sunny's file, was English, sweet sixteen, and still at school.

They were almost at the school now. 'Stanley Village,' said Janet as they passed a petrol station and followed the road round to the left.

'Looks nice,' said Wise from the back seat. Then he frowned. 'Thought you said it was by the sea?'

'It is.' Janet pointed to the left. 'There's a beach over there, can't move for swimmers in summer. And down there', she added as she pointed to a road on the right, 'is the main street which also gives on to the sea. Stanley's in a sort of bottle-neck. Water on both sides.'

'Expensive?' Despite the nature of their mission, Wise was clearly in holiday mode.

Janet shrugged. 'This *is* Hong Kong. Nothing's cheap.' Then, passing a row of shops, she indicated to the right. 'St Hilda's School is up here.'

Beside her, Fitz grinned as he noticed the name of the road they were turning into. 'Wong Ma Kok Road,' he said loudly.

Janet shot him an irritated glance. Was it just the broad Scottish accent, or had he deliberately emphasized the third word? His blank expression told her nothing. Then, suddenly, he turned round and winked at her. Janet glared back. Pathetic, that's what it was. And very British.

St Hilda's School for Young Ladies was also very British. While the original gothic monstrosity had been demolished and an equally hideous modern structure built in its place, the Victorian spirit lived on in the uniforms of the pupils. The girls making their way from one lesson to another in the forecourt as they drove up were dressed identically in white pinafores with blue mariner bows at the front. Socks and 'sensible' shoes completed the ensemble.

'Christ!' said Fitz as Janet drew to a halt. 'Whose idea was that? They look like bloody penguins.'

'Probably feel like them too.' Janet switched off the ignition and opened her door. She looked at the gaggle of schoolgirls in front of them. By far the majority were Chinese; there were only a few European faces. Janet wondered if Catherine Wilson was among them.

She wasn't. The headmistress, forewarned of their arrival and their purpose, had already ensconced her in the school office. Tight-lipped and censorious, Miss Henderson was deeply suspicious about the police wanting to question one of 'her girls': it wasn't the sort of thing that happened at St Hilda's.

'Catherine', she said after the three visitors had found their way to her office and introduced themselves, 'is waiting for you. May I ask', she added over the rim of her bi-focals, 'what this is about? I really can't have the police traipsing in here all the time, you know. Not very good for the school's image.'

Just wait, thought Fitz, until Catherine Wilson's pregnancy begins to show.

'It's purely a routine matter,' answered Janet. 'We think Catherine may be able to help us with an investigation. Not', she added hastily, 'that she's done anything wrong. We think she may be able to help identify someone, that's all.'

Miss Henderson's response, a dismissive snort, indicated that she didn't believe that was 'all'. 'Catherine', she said, pointing towards the corridor, 'is waiting for you in the room opposite. I trust you won't keep her long.'

'No. Just a few minutes. Thank you.' Janet turned on her heel, the men meekly following. All three felt inches smaller, decades younger. All three sighed with relief when the door closed behind them.

Catherine had known the moment she had been summoned. Someone had found out about her; the game was up. But why the *police*? She wasn't under age. Nor was Greg. She hadn't committed any crime. She sat, quaking with terror, waiting for her interrogation.

But an inquisition was the last thing on Janet's mind. Fitz, too, oozed sympathy the minute he entered the room and saw the slender, auburn-blond schoolgirl, hands neatly clasped in her lap – and looking hardly a day over fourteen. Affable as ever, Wise bellowed a cheery 'Hiya, love', as Janet introduced him. Catherine's fear lessened perceptibly. Whatever these people wanted, it wasn't to berate her. And then, suddenly, she remembered Dr Sunny.

'It's about him, isn't it?' she asked in a clear, very English voice as Janet sat down beside her. 'About Dr Sunny?'

'Yes.'

'You found my name in his records?'

'Yes.'

'Oh.' Catherine lowered her head and twisted her hands in her lap. 'When I read about the murder', she sniffed, 'I didn't know what to do.' Then she looked up again, a hint of desperation in her eyes. 'I'm nearly four months already.'

Janet's heart went out to the girl. Finding herself

unable to say anything, she reached for Catherine's hand.

'Your parents don't know?' asked Fitz.

Catherine shook her head. 'My parents work for the government and . . .'

'Your boyfriend?' he prompted.

Again a shake of the head. 'He's a student teacher. He's . . .' Catherine faltered into silence, yet the direction of her glance told them exactly who he was. A hockey match was in progress on the pitch outside. The players, some giggling and others deadly serious, were being coached by a young, handsome Chinese instructor.

Janet gave Catherine's hand a reassuring squeeze and then withdrew her own. Extracting a notebook from her handbag, she flicked through the pages. 'Okay, Catherine, this won't take long. Your last appointment with the doctor', she read, 'was two p.m. on the 17th?'

'Yes. No. Well . . . I went back later. I was on my way back to school, but I realized I'd left my bag. I used a handbag', she added with a small smile, 'to make me look older.'

Janet's heart was racing. 'You went back to the surgery? You saw Dr Sunny?'

'Yes. He was with a patient.' Janet and Fitz exchanged glances. According to the appointment book, there was no patient. Catherine's appointment had been the last of the day. 'I got the bag,' continued Catherine, 'and left.' Aware of the sudden tension around her, she added, a touch defiantly, that she hadn't seen the man's face, 'not really'.

'Man?' Fitz pounced on the word.

'An Englishman. His back was to me.'

'Why *English?*' pressed Fitz. 'Why not white, Caucasian?'

The question surprised Catherine. 'Oh! I . . . I don't know. Maybe I picked out a word or an accent before I knocked.'

'Could you identify him?'

Catherine looked doubtful. 'Fair hair,' she ventured. 'He had a briefcase on his knee.' Then, frowning, she turned to Janet.

'Is he the one who . . . who . . .?'

'We don't know, Catherine. We're following every lead at the moment.' Yet privately, for Catherine's sake, she hoped he wasn't their man. The poor girl didn't stand much of a chance keeping her pregnancy from her parents if she were questioned again or, worse, called to an identity parade.

It was as if Catherine sensed her thoughts. Suddenly fearful again, she whirled round. 'Promise me you won't say anything to my dad. *Please.*'

Janet nodded and stood up. 'What will you do, Catherine?'

Catherine hung her head. 'I don't know.'

To the surprise of the two men, Janet suddenly leaned down and hugged Catherine. She didn't say anything; the gesture was enough. And it was enough to confirm to Fitz that Janet Lee Cheung empathized totally with the girl, that she had been there before her.

*

'Lunch?' asked Wise as, having taken their leave and bade a relieved farewell to Miss Henderson, they sped through Stanley and past an inviting-looking restaurant.

Janet shook her head. 'There's an apple in the glove-compartment if you're hungry,' she said with a grin. 'We've got work to do.'

Fitz looked at the list of names in his lap. 'How long will it take us to get through all these people?'

'Ages, probably. Most of them are *Tai Tais* and . . .'

'*Tai Tais?*'

'Ladies who lunch. They've got everything except something to do. You never know,' she said over her shoulder to Wise, 'one of them may offer us lunch.'

One of them did. Their next port of call was a sumptuous villa in Shek-O, the home of one Dolly Poon. Mrs Poon, explained the manservant who answered the door, was taking lunch on the terrace. Would they care to join her?

'No,' replied Janet, avoiding Wise's outraged glare. 'We won't be a minute.'

But they were many minutes with Dolly Poon – and with the other five ladies they managed to interview that day. All of them had had appointments with Dr Sunny the day after his murder, and, without exception, they made it quite clear that they thought Dr Sunny extremely inconsiderate in getting himself killed. And all of them had theories as to why he had died. One lady, even richer and more petulant than Dolly Poon, ventured that Dr Sunny was a mere pawn in a greater game that in fact revolved around herself. His murder had been a warning to her. She would be next.

None of the ladies knew anything about a fair-haired Englishman. And none of them expressed the slightest sorrow over Dr Sunny's grieving widow and three children.

The day left all three of them feeling frustrated. Wise, claiming low blood sugar and the need to 'eat a bloody horse', clocked off early to eat at the hotel. Fitz accompanied Janet back to the police station and then, at eight o'clock, suggested they go out to dinner.

Janet looked doubtful. 'Ellison's complaining about how much we're spending on you.'

'I'll pay for dinner, then.'

Janet laughed. 'That's not exactly what I meant.'

'Well, it's exactly what *I* meant. Where can we go that's not . . .?'

'Too expensive?'

'Too noisy.'

Grinning, aware that expense was indeed the issue, Janet stood up. She knew just the place. And anyway, she would pay. Ellison was beginning to annoy her. Fitz, on the other hand, was beginning to intrigue her.

She took him to Tables 88 in Lan Kwai Fong. Unlike Su-Lin Tang, Janet enjoyed the buzz of the area, liked the 'happening' atmosphere and the people who were a far cry both from the Dolly Poons of this world and the hapless illegal immigrants who took up so much of her time.

Fitz liked the wine. He demolished most of the first

169

bottle even before the food arrived and, eyes lighting up as his steak was brought to him, waved it in the waiter's face. 'We'll have another of this when you're ready.'

Janet looked at him over the rim of her own barely touched glass. What made him tick, she wondered? This big, brash man with his moody silences and angry outbursts. What was his home-life like? His wife, his children? What were the grudges that he seemed to harbour? She suspected she would never know: she had seen Fitz in action enough to know that he took and didn't give.

Fitz leaned towards her. 'Have you ever said it?'

Startled out of her reverie, Janet nearly dropped her glass.

'Said what?'

'Have you never cracked, pinned him to the wall and told him what an arsehole he is?'

'Who?'

Fitz waved a dismissive hand. 'You know who. Ellison.'

Janet paused before replying. 'That's not my opinion,' she lied. 'You just don't like him.'

'And you do? The Brit with no talent in your job? Janet, that's loyalty on the verge of self-abuse.' Grinning, Fitz waved a finger in front of her. 'That's a bad English habit you've picked up.'

Janet toyed with a tiger prawn on her plate. 'I can think of worse,' she said with a slow smile.

But Fitz was now looking intently at her. Suddenly she felt alarmed, as if she had been keeping things from him and that he knew it. 'Your parents wouldn't agree with that,' he said. 'They had bigger plans for you. You had to put up a fight to join the police force.'

Damn the man, thought Janet. How does he know? How can he tell? She looked at him, impassive, giving nothing away.

Fitz continued to stare. Doesn't she realize, he wondered, that she oozes class? The Ivy-League accent, the poise? The understated, expensive clothes? 'What does your father do?' he asked.

'He's a stockbroker.'

'Taught you English from the year dot.'

A slow smile spread across Janet's face. 'I was taught lots of languages.' The American tutor, she recalled. The Swiss finishing school. The year in Japan. And then the police force. No wonder her father thought he had wasted his money.

'You live', said Fitz, 'in an English colony.' He gestured at their fellow diners. 'Surrounded by 18-carat Englishness. Yet your father chose to have you tutored in the Language of Opportunity by an American? What does he think of Gordon and Tonic Ellison?'

Janet knew her father thought Ellison was FILTH. The epitome of opportunism. A loser. And a bully. But how dare Fitz, a visitor in a land he could never understand, dissect her life. 'At least Ellison's honest,' she said. 'The worst Europeans are the ones who have the strong opinions about what other Europeans are doing here.'

Fitz just laughed. 'A fly-by lecture tour's not an invasive occupation. Unless I fart "Land of Hope and Glory" over a seminar on white-collar crime. Which I hope I've grown out of.'

Despite herself, Janet laughed with him. Then, in an attempt to keep the conversation away from herself, he asked him if he often did lecture tours.

There was nothing studied about Fitz's vehement response. 'No. This is my first and last.' He stabbed at the steak in front of him. 'Plane full of wanky academics flying round the world thinking they're on a mercy dash. "We have to swap cultures,"' he intoned, curling his lip in disgust at the memory. 'Christ, there's more bloody culture in a pasteurized yoghurt.'

'So you were happy when we came along?'

Yes, thought Fitz, I bloody well was. Despite the fact that you behaved like a stuck-up cow. He raised his glass. 'Not as happy as my wife's going to be. Scunthorpe!'

'Scunthorpe?' Janet's hand was hesitant on her glass.

'It's where my wife's from.'

Oh, thought Janet. But where's Jane Penhaligon from?

Fitz drank most of the second bottle of wine as well. Then he had a brandy. Then he went back to the hotel and raided the minibar. Tomorrow was going to be another *Tai Tai* day. Their first appointment was at the house of one Su-Lin Tang. Janet had told him over dinner that she lived in a smart block in Mid-Levels and that Miss Tang would have spent the last few days concocting theories about the murder of her doctor – all of which would no doubt revolve around her good self.

Chapter Seven

Su-Lin Tang was not at home when they called. When they arrived at the luxurious penthouse in Happy Valley, she was dangling in mid-air, still trapped in the crate, battered and bruised and being tossed around as a fork-lift truck lifted her prison. Her agonized screams for help were drowned out by the noise of the truck's engine; her remaining bottles of water spilled their contents all over the floor and both her fan and her torch crashed into lifelessness as they were hurled against the wall of the crate. When the crate was lowered to its new home, it was just as well that Su-Lin couldn't see what was happening. The driver of the truck had positioned it between two other containers, with the door pressed firmly against the unyielding metal of one of them. Then he reversed his vehicle and drove off to pick up the next crate – the one that he would put on top of Su-Lin's.

But all Janet's team knew was that Su-Lin was not at home. 'We're looking', said Janet to the elderly lady who answered their knock on the door, 'for Su-Lin Tang.'

The lady, already looking distinctly worried, became even more alarmed at the sight of the ID Janet flashed at her. Wide-eyed, she stared at the three visitors. 'Gone,' she said. 'Su-Lin's gone. Not here.'

'Are you', asked Janet in Cantonese, 'her mother?'

Wei Wei nodded. This was worse than she had thought. Her daughter had disappeared without telling anyone – and now the police were looking for her. What had she done? And why? And why had she disappeared in such a hurry? Arriving at the flat at a time when she knew Dennis would be absent, Wei Wei had searched through her daughter's belongings in the bedroom. Most of them were still there. The two new dresses Dennis had bought her were still hanging in the wardrobe – and most of her cosmetics were still in the bathroom. If there was one thing Wei Wei knew about Su-Lin, it was how fastidious she was.

'Do you live with your daughter,' asked Janet, nudging the older woman out of her reverie.

'No.' Then she opened the door further and invited them in. 'I'm just visiting. Come,' she said. 'I'll show you. I think something's happened to her.'

Fitz and Janet exchanged a half-worried, half-triumphant look and followed her into the apartment and down the corridor into the bedroom. Wise, behind them, lingered in the large living-room.

Still fearful but suddenly animated, Wei Wei threw open the doors of the fitted wardrobe. 'She leaves him,' she said, nodding to herself. 'She runs away. Fine. But this,' she said, pointing to the dresses. 'And this – she bought them only last week. Why take only old clothes? And why doesn't she phone me? Me! It makes no sense.'

Fitz was looking at something else that, to him, didn't make sense either. It was a nightlight beside the bed: not a reading light, the angle was wrong. And anyway, he discovered as he bent to examine it, it was too low-powered. All it would provide was a gentle glow all night long. Fitz had seen an identical one at the bedside of his daughter when she had been tiny and afraid of the dark. That had made sense, and Katie had grown out of it. But why would a grown man – or indeed, a grown woman – be scared of the dark? Then, shrugging, he turned to Janet. 'Ask her', he whispered, 'when she actually left.'

'Tuesday,' answered Wei Wei herself.

Fitz nodded. 'Ah. Before the murder.'

'Murder?' Wei Wei's eyes widened in horror. 'What murder?'

'Dr Sunny. You know him?'

Wei Wei had never met him – but she'd seen him, seen the photograph in the newspaper of the body slumped against the car tyre. She nodded. 'But what's Dr Sunny got to do with Su-Lin?'

Oh God, thought Janet, she doesn't know about the baby.

'You didn't know', asked Fitz, 'that she was pregnant?'

Wei Wei's astonished gasp was answer enough. She

175

looked, disbelieving, at her visitors. Then, overwhelmed by the events of the last few minutes, she sat on the bed and put her head in her hands.

'She consulted the doctor', said Fitz gently, 'about a termination.'

But Wei Wei didn't understand the last word. Janet translated for her.

'No.' The vehemence of Wei Wei's response surprised them both. 'Never. Not that. *He*', she said, 'would never allow.'

'Her boyfriend?'

A flame of hatred burned in Wei Wei's eyes. 'Yes. Dennis.'

Janet looked as if she had been hit. 'Den . . .?'

But she was cut short by Charlie Wise, bounding into the room. His snooping had paid dividends. In his hand he was holding a framed photograph of a smiling Su-Lin and an equally happy-looking Dennis Philby. But Wise was looking anything but happy; he looked as if he had seen a ghost. 'You do know', he said, thrusting the photograph under Janet's nose, 'whose house we're in?'

Janet put both hands to her mouth in horror. She was recalling the instruction she had written to herself the other night. *Find out Dennis Philby's home address.* Dennis Philby, towards whom she had rather warmed. Dennis Philby, who lived with Su-Lin Tang – who had been seeing Dr Sunny. Dennis Philby, the connection between the two murdered men.

*

Dennis was delighted with the way things were going. The wedding had, he reckoned, been the most moving experience of his life. Su-Lin, too, had been overwhelmed with joy. He had wanted to stay with her, to make love with her at the end of that momentous evening, but had steeled himself to leave. He had big plans for their first night as man and wife; they would spend it in altogether more luxurious surroundings. It would be a night they would never forget.

Dennis bounded up the steps of Immigration Tower, certain and confident in his purpose. Temple Street Market had served him well last night. As well as the wedding dress, the candles and the ring, he had indeed located, in a tiny stall behind the fortune tellers, the batch of certificates. Years ago, when he had first arrived in the Far East, someone had told him that you could buy anything, absolutely anything you wanted in Hong Kong – provided you were prepared to pay for it. He grinned as he entered the building and trotted across the lobby towards the lifts. Strictly speaking, he hadn't paid for anything he'd bought last night. Peter Yang had.

His appointment was for ten forty-five with a man called Gerald Freeman. That was a stroke of luck: Dennis recalled meeting the man barely a month ago at some function or other. Freeman would no doubt remember him as well. The omens were good.

Freeman's memory, however, wasn't as good as Dennis's. When, five minutes later, Dennis was called into his office on the fourteenth floor, the other man

177

introduced himself, evidently under the impression that they hadn't met before.

'Dennis Philby?' he asked, rising from behind his desk and holding out a hand. 'Gerald Freeman.'

Dennis took the proffered hand and shook it with a vigour that surprised Freeman. 'We've met,' he said, smiling broadly.

Freeman frowned. 'Have we?'

'Yes. Martin Lee's birthday party down at the Correspondents' Club.' Following Freeman's lead, Dennis sat down on the visitor's side of the desk. 'Octoberish?'

Freeman heard the note of censure in Dennis's voice. He chose to ignore it. There was, he decided, something about this man he didn't like. He was altogether too bouncy, too boyishly confident. 'You're a friend of Martin's, then?' he said, mustering a smile.

'You kidding?' laughed Dennis. 'We're like brothers.' He smiled across the table in what to Freeman was an irritatingly familiar manner. No doubt Philby thought he was well on the way to establishing another sibling relationship.

'So . . .?'

'Your wife,' interrupted Dennis, 'she's . . . something big in the legal-eagle world?'

'You've a good memory.'

'She all right? Kids all right?'

'No kids.'

Dennis laughed. 'Right! Not that good a memory, then!'

'So . . . er, what can I do for you?' Under the desk, Freeman was gently tapping his foot.

So, maniacally, was Dennis. He only stopped when he reached down for his briefcase, placed it in his lap and, still smiling, opened it. Then, with a triumphant flourish, he produced his marriage certificate and handed it over to Freeman.

The other man groaned inwardly. He wondered if Philby had any idea how many times this happened; how many times he found himself sitting opposite bumptious Englishmen who thought that the act of producing a marriage certificate entitled the new, Chinese wife to a British passport. Freeman didn't even have to look at the name of Philby's spouse to know that she would be Chinese. They always were. Nor did he have to look too closely at the certificate to know that it was fake.

His face betraying no emotion, Freeman looked up at Dennis. Did this man know that it was fake? Was that why he was here, to request a genuine replacement? Freeman doubted it. Dennis, like all the others, was after the passport. 'I don't', he said cautiously, 'know what you want me to say?'

The first flash of doubt crossed Dennis's features. 'Well,' he said with a nervous grin, '"Congratulations" wouldn't go amiss! It's taken me long enough to persuade her. Mrs Dennis Philby.' Articulating Su-Lin's new name pleased him, relaxed him. 'Sounds really weird, I'll tell you.'

'Mmm. Well, the thing is . . .'

'She needs a passport. You just say "yes", don't you?'

179

Freeman exhaled deeply. How old was this man, he wondered? His own age? A little younger? Old enough, anyway, to know better. 'About a year ago,' he began, 'a batch of marriage certificates disappeared from the printers.' He tapped at the certificate in front of him. 'They're selling for . . . oh, around twenty thousand dollars. Maybe thirty. This isn't even a good copy. I've seen them for sale myself down at Temple Street, for God's sake. But', he added, smiling without humour, 'do you know what the joke is?'

Dennis's eyes narrowed. There were no jokes as far as he was concerned. This was deadly serious.

But Freeman didn't notice the anger in the cold blue eyes. 'This copy', he said, waving the offending item in front of Dennis, 'isn't even worth the paper it's printed on. It's pointless, Dennis. The only passports issued were to High Yield Emigrés – "Hyenas" if you're being cynical.' For the first time, Freeman felt a twinge of pity for the man opposite him. Mrs Dennis Philby, for all he knew, was equally deserving of a passport as the hyenas. But the biggest cynics of them all, the British Government, had put paid to her chances long ago. 'The UK', he continued, 'tried to make it look like refugee rescue but the only status they've targeted since Patten pitched camp was big business. If you were on the list, Dennis,' he finished with weary exasperation, 'you wouldn't be here now.'

But Dennis *was* here, and he wasn't going to accept defeat. 'Look,' he said, also leaning forward. 'I'm a British citizen. I want a passport for my wife.'

'If this is all you've got, she is not your wife.'

It was the wrong thing to say. Dennis's eyes turned to steel.

'I married Su-Lin Tang yesterday and it's my bloody right to take her to England with me. Why's that a problem for you?'

For the first time, Freeman began to feel uneasy. He was used to dealing with angry people, upset people, bolshie British citizens who thought their passports entitled them to the world. But there was something different about Dennis.

'Look,' he said, handing the certificate back, 'calm down. I should', he added as he stood up, 'be notifying the police now. I won't.'

Dennis didn't take the hint.

Freeman forced a smile. 'Turn round and go, and we'll forget I ever saw the stuff, okay?'

'Twenty grand in cash.'

'I didn't hear that,' said Freeman with all the patience he could muster.

'Thirty.'

Freeman finally lost his temper. 'This is my job! If . . .'

'Forty. Please. Forty.'

'I'm trying', shouted Freeman, pointing towards the door, 'to do you a big bloody favour here, and really, the most sensible thing you could do right now is just *piss off*, okay?'

Dennis stood up. 'Okay, okay. I'm going.' He took one step towards the door and then, hearing Freeman's sigh of relief, turned and swung the briefcase.

The blow, or possibly the other crack to the head when he hit the corner of the desk, killed Freeman. All Dennis cared about was the fact that the man died so quickly. It made the task of binding his hands in prayer so much swifter.

Janet acted with alacrity. Within minutes of seeing the photograph of Dennis Philby and Su-Lin Tang, she was on the phone to headquarters. Mere moments after that, a general alert was issued to the entire Hong Kong Police Force. It contained Dennis Philby's description, his age and his height, details and the registration of his BMW – and the reasons why he was wanted. When the alert was issued, there were three reasons: suspicion of the murders of Peter Yang and Dr Sunny and of the abduction of Su-Lin Tang.

Half an hour later, they added a forth. Gerald Freeman's body was found, bound and gagged, by his assistant. The gag, like that of Dr Sunny, was unusual. It was a crumpled marriage certificate.

'Jesus!' said Wise when they heard the news. 'He married her? *Yesterday?*'

But Janet knew better. Like every law-enforcer in Hong Kong, she knew of the existence of the fake certificates. 'Check', she said down the mobile to Benny Ho, 'the serial number. Odds are it's a Temple Street certificate.' Then, eyes blazing, she switched off her phone and turned to Fitz. 'We've got him!'

'Have we?' Fitz was more sanguine. 'It isn't over till the fat lady sings.'

'What?' Janet's cosmopolitan education hadn't embraced such eclecticism.

Fitz shrugged. 'We know *who* our man is – but not where.'

'We'll find him.' Janet was back in the driving seat, literally and figuratively. She was in charge – and they roared through the streets on their way to the offices of Philby Medical. Above and behind them, a police helicopter soared into the sky – one of three involved in the search.

None of them expected Dennis to be at work. None of them was disappointed. They were met by a weary-looking Fiona Chang. She had intended to hand in her notice that day, and had been thwarted. There was no one for her to give notice to.

'Where's Dennis Philby?' barked Janet, once again flashing her ID.

'He's not in today. I don't know where he is.' Fitz, Wise and Janet all read the 'I don't care either' implicit in her tone.

Undaunted, Janet led the way into Dennis's tiny office. Below them, a police car with two more officers and two forensics experts screeched to a halt. Janet was taking no chances; she wanted every item dusted for fingerprints; every document found and examined.

To her annoyance, Fitz sat down at Philby's desk and, as if he hadn't a care in the world, stared out of the window. 'Philby Medical,' he said to the room in general, 'what do they do?'

'Export things,' snapped Janet. 'Or rather, they used

to. Philby's lawyers have just filed a bankruptcy order.'
She pointed to a shipping certificate pinned to the
notice-board.

'So he's used to transporting things out of the country?'

'You could say that.'

'By ship or by air?'

'Both.'

'So if he's intending to take the girlfriend out of the
country . . .?'

'He won't have a chance by air. Detective Ho has just
alerted Kai Tak.'

'But by sea?'

Janet turned, exhaled deeply, and looked Fitz in the
eye. She wished he hadn't asked the question. She knew
that Hong Kong was the busiest port on earth; that
people shipped goods all over the world every hour and
minute, all day and all night. She also knew that a huge
proportion of the cargoes were unregistered; that illegal,
smuggled goods slipped silently past the harbour police
and out into the waters of the world with horrifying re-
gularity. And Janet knew, as the others did not, that
Hong Kong was comprised of over two hundred rocks
and islands. That meant thousands of coves, thousands
of sampans bobbing in the quiet waters, thousands of
junks chugging from island to island. Hundreds of ways
to conceal cargo – alive or dead.

'We'll find him,' said Janet. 'And we'll find her. No
way can they leave the country.' She wished she could
have said the words with more conviction. Fitz plainly
didn't believe them. Nor did she.

When they returned to the police station, Charlie Wise phoned England. He was busy for more than an hour. So, in Happy Valley, was Benny Ho. Under Janet's instructions, he searched every inch of Dennis Philby's apartment. His activities were not in vain. Nor were Wise's. He discovered that Fitz had been right, after all, about a certain childhood spent in Romford, Essex.

Dennis was on his way back to Kowloon. He had already forgotten about Gerald Freeman. Civil servants had always come low in his estimation and Freeman had been one of the lowest. He had been an irrelevance, an inconvenient blip in the time-clock of Dennis's great plan. A plan that, passport or not, was about to come to fruition. Dennis drove towards the Eastern Tunnel, exceeding the speed limit, unaware of the irony that, should he be caught, he wouldn't be booked for speeding.

As he approached the tunnel entrance, a police helicopter roared overhead. Dennis didn't see it: its occupants didn't see Dennis. The silver BMW, licence plate FV 7872, disappeared from view. The helicopter remained on the island side of the water. Janet Lee Cheung had not yet extended the search to Kowloon.

Twenty minutes later Dennis was in a blind panic. He had driven, as usual, as near as he could to Su-Lin's crate and then walked the rest of the way. At first he thought he had made a wrong turning, that he had been too pre-occupied with his plan to remember the route through the maze of crates. Then, forcing himself to concentrate,

185

he looked at the containers in front of him. The blue one with the Australian registration was still here. So was the other Philby Medical one, the empty one. But beside it there was now a space. And in front of the space were the tyre marks of a fork-lift truck. Apart from that, there was nothing and no one. He was alone and Su-Lin had gone.

Then the stillness was interrupted by the mechanical whine of a crane. More noise, the incessant Hong Kong noise that Dennis had begun to detest. Never, he raged, was he allowed to be alone, to be quiet. And then he remembered that with the noise came the light and the reasons why he liked that. Even at night, there was always light. Forcing himself to be calm, gulping deep breaths, he looked, frowning, at the empty space. Someone had moved the crate: that was allowed. It was supposed to be empty and, according to the shipping yard's regulations, could therefore be moved to make way for containers that needed to be unloaded. The shipping office would be able to tell him where it was.

And then he thought of his Su-Lin, of the terror she must have felt at being lifted, swung in the air and transported to another location. Had she been hurt? He knew how the crates were thrown around. Had the baby been hurt? Panicking again, he ran down the aisle of crates. 'Su-Lin!' he yelled. 'Su-Lin! I'm here! I'm coming!' His voice, defeated by the ranks of vast containers and the noise of the crane, echoed feebly around the basin.

Then he saw it. His crate. Su-Lin's little home. It was at the end of a row, wedged between two others and underneath another. Panting, he ran towards it and flung himself against the hard metal surface. He didn't notice that the side of the crate was completely flush, that there were no hinges, no door. 'Su-Lin!' he screamed. 'It's okay! It's all right! I'm here.'

Su-Lin heard him. Aware that she was now severely dehydrated, hurting in every limb and drifting in and out of consciousness, she thought she was hallucinating. Then, willing herself into wakefulness, she heard the voice again. It didn't matter that it was the voice of the man who had imprisoned her, of the Dennis she had once loved and now feared and hated. All that mattered was the contact. Somebody knew where she was.

Only a few tiny chinks of light penetrated the terrible blackness of the crate. The air, still and rank, was in equally short supply. But somehow Su-Lin, perspiring and gasping with the effort, blundering in the dark, managed to claw her way to the front of the crate and the source of the voice. Her own voice came in a hoarse, desperate and barely audible rasp. 'Dennis!' she moaned as she clawed at the unyielding metal. 'Dennis! Please help me . . . *please*. I can't breathe. I can't last much longer. *Please!*'

'Don't worry!' yelled Dennis. 'We'll be together, I promise you! I love you. I'm coming back!' The last words were fainter. To Su-Lin's befuddled mind, they seemed more distant, as if spoken from afar. And then, when there was no reply to her next, anguished wail, she realized what had happened. Dennis had established she was alive. In his mind he had thought she was all right.

187

He had gone. And then he would come back. And then there would be some other fresh horror to torment her.

Su-Lin's legs gave way beneath her. She had already shed her tears, sobbed her screams: now there was nothing left. She sank to the ground, neither noticing nor caring that she was collapsing into her own mess, into bits of orange peel and the accumulated detritus of the past few days. She was used to the stinking rubbish of her prison. She wondered, almost disinterestedly, how much her own body would smell when it too began to rot.

Dennis bounded away from the crate. Positive again, relieved that Su-Lin had not suffered when the crate had been moved, he had only one thought in his desperate mind: to prepare for the journey to England. How many supplies would he need, he wondered as he ran to his car? How many crates of water for the six-week journey? How many clothes? He smiled to himself as he leaped into the BMW and gunned the engine. A sea voyage. Su-Lin liked the sea. And it would be good for the baby; the calm lapping of the water against the sides of the ship. It didn't cross his mind, even for one second, that a sea voyage would kill Su-Lin. It didn't occur to him that she would be knocked around far more than she had been in the cargo basin; that if she didn't die from injuries she would suffocate, starve or die from dehydration. The voyage, now that the passport was no longer a possibility, was the only way he could get her to England. And, because *he* had thought of it, it would be all right.

He stopped the car outside the shipping office at the

entrance of the cargo basin. Leaving the engine running, he hurried into the building and into the chief clerk's room. The little man looked up at him without surprise or even much interest. Dennis Philby's comings and goings were regular occurrences.

Dennis slapped an export ID card on the desk. 'I've a shipment ready to move.'

'Yes?'

'Yes. Over there.' Dennis jabbed a finger in the direction of the red crate. 'Philby Medical PM356. End of aisle three.'

'But those crates are empty! We moved them yesterday!'

'Well, you bloody well moved the wrong one! That crate', he yelled, 'is not empty! I have to get it on tomorrow's ten o'clock to Southampton!'

'But . . . !'

'Just move it, will you! Isn't that what I pay you people for?'

Dennis stormed out of the office before the clerk could reply. He stood and watched the irate Englishman leap into his car and tear out onto the road. Then he shrugged and went back to his comic. Dennis Philby's crate could wait.

Dennis's mood changed again as he drove back in the direction of the tunnel. Now that his preparations were almost complete, he needed to be cautious. He mustn't leave room for anything to go wrong at the last minute. He must be calm.

It was the calmness that saved him. Driving sedately

back to Philby Medical to pick up his own passport, he saw the police car before its occupants saw him. Never before had he seen a police car outside his business premises. It was a boring area, quiet for Hong Kong. Nothing ever happened there: no crime, that was for sure. There could be only one reason for the police presence. They had caught up with him.

With a coolness that surprised him, Dennis eased the car into reverse, turned the corner and joined the heavy traffic heading towards Wanchai. He wondered, briefly, how they had found him. Then he found he didn't care enough to be alarmed. Somewhere in the back of his mind, a voice was telling him that he wanted to be caught. No: not caught. Stopped. He didn't really like the killing. But he did need to be with Su-Lin. And she needed supplies. He could get them in Wanchai market.

He parked the car, illegally again, and rushed towards the jumble of little roadside stalls. Oranges, he said to himself. Oranges were the first priority. And folic acid. That, he had read, was a must for pregnant women. Then he remembered that the previous can of capsules was still in his pocket. He had forgotten to give them to Su-Lin. Poor girl. That made his mission even more urgent. Buttonholing a startled stallkeeper, he barked his order in Cantonese. The wizened man, used to the peculiarities of *gweilos*, shrugged and reached for a carrier bag and began to count out thirty oranges.

And then Dennis's luck ran out. Standing beside the stallholder, barely able to contain his irritation at the man's slowness, he began to tap his foot. Then, to stop himself hitting the man, he looked away – and locked eyes with the policeman. He knew, instantly, what was happening: the policeman's nod as he spoke into his radio confirmed it.

Dennis didn't hesitate. Ignoring the huge bag of oranges he was being proffered, he broke into a run. Knocking over the neighbouring stall, sending fruit and vegetables flying, he pelted down the street.

The policeman was younger, fitter and leaner than Dennis. He sprinted after him, ducking and diving as he chased his prey through the market. He was gaining by the second. Then, as Dennis turned a corner, he grinned and slowed his pace. Dennis had gone into a tiny cul-de-sac. He stood and watched him for a moment. When Dennis turned back, realizing his mistake, he found himself looking down the barrel of the policeman's gun.

Chapter Eight

Gordon Ellison was grinning like a Cheshire cat. Everything was falling into place. The only thing that still troubled him was his earlier panic about this case. He couldn't imagine what had got into him: couldn't believe that he had confided his worries to Janet. It was embarrassing; undignified. But more undignified was the fact that he had let himself be talked into hiring this fat psychologist and his shorter, yet still rotund, sidekick.

He bestowed a benign, yet distinctly superior, smile on Janet.

'I think', he purred, 'we're beyond civilian assistance now, don't you?'

Janet looked as if she had been hit. 'What?'

So did Fitz. 'Me?'

'Yes. Thank you very much, Dr Fitzgerald. Enjoy the

money. Oh . . . and it's been a pleasure meeting you.'

Janet stared, appalled, at her boss. 'I thought', she managed to stammer, 'he was a participant?'

Ellison shot her a condescending smile. 'Measured by what? His results?' He looked at Fitz who had, to his mind, achieved precisely nothing except a large bill at the Ritz Carlton. 'Or', he added nastily, 'his money?'

Wise looked at Fitz. He was, he thought, taking all this extremely calmly. Probably, he reasoned correctly, because Fitz wasn't taking it seriously. He knew he was needed.

Fitz shrugged, affecting complete insouciance. His words, however, belied his manner. 'You only know it's him because he ran. He only ran because he was being chased. And the only thing you've got to link him to his victims is his girlfriend – who isn't here. Good luck, Gordon.' Then he stepped towards the door. 'Where's the canteen again?'

Janet would have clapped had she not been aware of the seriousness of the situation. She held out a hand, indicating for Fitz to stop. 'You stay,' she said, glaring at Ellison.

Ellison merely looked amused. 'Bit early for a cultural coup, isn't it, Janet?'

Ouch, thought Wise. Way below the belt.

'If he goes,' replied the policewoman, 'I go.' Then, without waiting for a reply from the astounded Ellison, she stalked out of the room, gesturing for Fitz and Wise to follow. Totally wrong-footed, Ellison stared after her. He became positively enraged when he saw where Janet was heading. Without a backward glance, not caring what Ellison thought of her or even seeking his permission, she went straight into the interview room at the end of the corridor. The two British men followed her.

Janet's rage served her well when she sat down opposite Dennis Philby. As Wise closed the door of the interview room, she crossed her legs and leaned back in her chair. The glacial coolness of her eyes and the immobility of her face contradicted the relaxed body language.

Dennis tried, unsuccessfully, to hide his own nervousness. He puffed on a cigarette, looked at the light-fitting, tapped his non-existent ash. Still Janet didn't move a muscle. Wise and Fitz, flanking her like minders, accentuated her aura of power.

Dennis couldn't stand the silence any longer. 'You shouldn't even be talking to me', he said as he ground his cigarette into the ashtray, 'without my lawyer.'

'We'll get you a duty lawyer.'

'I don't want a duty lawyer. Willy Teng's my lawyer. I want him here.'

'Calm down,' said Wise. 'We haven't even asked you anything yet.'

But they were about to. 'Why', asked Janet, 'did you run from the policeman in Wanchai?'

Dennis lit another cigarette. 'Because he was chasing me with a gun. Call it instinct. I don't know about you, but I tend to value my life.'

'But not Peter Yang's?' snapped Janet.

Dennis stared at her, inhaled, and then blew the

smoke straight across the table into her face. The gesture was as pathetic as it was insolent. 'We've been through all this before. Peter Yang was a friend.'

But Janet, since their last interview with Dennis, had been on the phone to Nancy Yang. Nancy had a different opinion of the relationship between Dennis Philby and her husband.

Sighing, Janet leaned forward and opened her notebook. 'Did you murder Peter Yang for money? He wrote you that cheque.'

'That was on Monday. Peter was killed on Tuesday.'

'The *date* on the cheque', said Wise, 'was Monday. Could've been written on Tuesday, eh?'

Dennis shrugged. Janet opened her handbag and produced a photocopy of the cheque. 'His wife confirms that his writing looks "strange". That's because the cheque was written under duress.'

'Rubbish.'

'Your dabs', said Wise, 'are on his chequebook.'

'Oh, I see.' Dennis leaned back in his chair and blew smoke at the ceiling. 'I'm being questioned for murder because I happened to hold somebody's chequebook?'

'No.' Fitz, also smoking, stepped forward. 'You're being questioned for murder because your girlfriend checked in with Dr Sunny for an abortion. Whom you also murdered in – and don't take this too personally – a manner befitting a man from Romford.'

'What?' Dennis felt he had been thrust onto a different pitch; pushed into a game with rules he didn't understand. He stared, surprised and uncomprehending, at Fitz.

'The only time I went to Romford,' explained Fitz for the benefit of all his listeners, 'I was chasing an undergraduate nymphomaniac whose parents were away – neither of which turned out to be true. There's me standing under her window, going "Ah, go on, Mitzi, giz a shag", and her dad came out the front door and smacked me.' As he finished, Fitz dragged a chair forward and plonked himself firmly down beside Dennis.

It was Dennis who broke the short – and on all sides, surprised – silence.

'Who', he said to Janet, 'is he?'

Fitz produced a business card and slammed it on the table beside Dennis. 'If you're ever passing through England, look me up,' he said kindly. 'I'll give you ten per cent off.'

But Dennis, peering at the card, had already decided that he never wanted to see Dr Edward Fitzgerald again. The words 'Criminal Psychologist' had a horrible, chilling effect on him.

'The discount', said Fitz, 'is on account of the fact that I already know pretty much how you tick. "Murders when provoked."' Fitz spat the words, accompanying them with a fist slamming down on top of his business card. 'Were you provoked, Dennis?'

'No.'

'Never? Never provoked?'

Dennis just looked. Where, he wondered, was this going? What was it all about, these stupid, odd questions.

He looked across to Janet and jabbed a thumb towards Fitz's substantial midriff.

'How much're you paying this joker?'

Still glacial, Janet just stared.

'You ever won anything, Dennis?' asked Fitz.

'Eh?'

'You murdered Peter Yang with a trophy. I'm wondering how significant that was?'

But Dennis chose not to enlighten him. Fitz didn't seem to mind. He had a barrage of surprises to throw at Dennis. Soon he wouldn't know what had hit him. 'Well,' he said, 'you're not one of eleven children, so where did all the competition come from?' Frowning, he put a hand to his forehead. 'Let me guess, Dennis. Only child I'd say. Son of a . . . builder? No, carpenter, more like.'

Dennis's eyes widened in shocked surprise.

'Mother's name,' continued Fitz, still playing the clairvoyant, 'begins with M. Mary? Maureen?' Then, startling the wits out of Dennis, he jumped round in his seat. 'No! I've got it! Gloria!'

Then he laughed and gave the confused Dennis a conspiratorial wink. 'I'm cheating, of course. I peeped at the notes', he said with a nod towards Wise, 'my colleague had faxed through from England. He's been talking to your family.'

Dennis was no longer cynical. Nor was he baffled or impressed. He was rigid with horror.

'What', he spat at Wise, 'have you said?'

'Me?' Wise shrugged as if he could hardly remember

the events of only an hour ago. 'Oh . . . nothing much. Three dead, blood everywhere and it's in all the papers . . . blah-di-blah.' Another shrug. 'As you do, y'know.'

Fitz pounced again before Dennis had even opened his mouth to protest. 'Working-class family,' he said. 'Middle of Romford. Only child. What', he asked Wise, 'is the family firm again?'

'Jack Philby and Co. Joiners.'

Fitz turned back to Dennis. 'Didn't fancy the business yourself, eh, Dennis?'

'No.'

'Couple of O Levels talk you out of it?'

'A Levels,' sneered Dennis. 'Three. Chemistry, Physics and Business Studies.'

'Business Studies!' Fitz roared with laughter. 'Bloody hell, Dennis!' In one swift move, he reached down for the plastic bag he had brought into the room with him: the bag containing the fruits of Benny Ho's search of the Happy Valley apartment. 'If these', he said, tipping the unpaid bills onto the table, 'aren't suing 'em for the course fees, I don't know what is!'

Dennis blanched.

'I wouldn't', remarked Wise, 'trust you with a bloody piggy bank, pal.'

Events were moving too quickly for Dennis now; the rules of the game were changing by the second. And then, out of the corner of his eye, he saw Janet pass another bag under the table to Fitz. When Fitz emptied its contents on top of the bills, Dennis realized that there was no game. This was an all-out attack.

'So,' said Fitz, looking at the jumble of photographs. 'There they are. Mum and Dad.'

Dennis's lower lip began to quiver. Fitz picked up the photograph he had been pointing at. 'In the back garden. In Romford. Essex. But', he added, 'you're having to tell your parents their lifestyle's not good enough for you. Your sights are sky high because you've flourished into . . .' Fitz paused and blew an imaginary trumpet '. . . an Educated Essex Boy! Once considered to be a contradiction in terms. How are the parents taking that?'

Dennis recoiled with distaste, trying to erect a barrier between himself and the brash, invasive presence on his left. 'He's proud of me.'

'He said that?'

'Yes.'

'Well, he lied. Your father's a skilled worker in a traditional occupation. What he wants more than anything else is the ritual of raising a child, setting him free, only to see him fly right back, stick to his father like shit on a blanket. Join the firm, take the wages, move two streets down. "I don't know what I'm doing wrong,"' intoned Fitz in a bad imitation of an Essex accent, '"I can't get rid of him." But inside he's singing, eh, Dennis? Huge compliment for a man like him.'

On the other side of the table, Janet found that her nails were digging into her palms.

But Dennis was anything but enraptured by Fitz's performance. Two high spots of colour appeared on his cheeks. 'Don't you dare', he spat, 'take the piss out of my father!'

'You did.'

'Wha . . .?'

'You must've.'

'What d'you mean? Oh, I *see*.' Back in sarcastic mode, Dennis curled his lip in distaste at the man beside him. 'You think my education was wasted? You're a middle-aged shrink and the best you can come up with is a few naff Essex jokes. Wow, you're really original.'

But Fitz knew that already. 'So,' he said, 'you're proud of Essex?'

'Yes.'

'The family?'

'Yes.'

'You love 'em so much, you chose to live six thousand miles away. A totally different life in totally the opposite direction, Dennis.' Fitz leaned closer, and stared into the younger man's eyes. 'Running from what, Dennis? Running from what?'

'Running from nothing.' Dennis shrugged. 'It was business.'

'A business that was doing so well you had to share it with the world?'

'If that's how you want to put it, yes.'

'No.' Fitz almost shouted the word, surprising Janet and Wise as well as Dennis. 'You came out here', he sneered, 'because your business collapsed. FILTH, Dennis. Failed in London, Try Hong Kong. You ran out here to escape your failure. You ran on failure. That's all right.' Suddenly Fitz smiled. 'That's half the Brits on the island.'

Dennis shook his head. 'Peter Yang persuaded me to

set up here because he knew we'd both make a bloody killing.'

'Pardon your Freudian French.' Fitz smiled again and, in a move that again surprised the others, stood up and went towards the door. But instead of opening it, he reached for the light switch and turned the dimmer to half power. The room, previously bright with the harsh light of interrogation, was now bathed in a softer, muted glow. Fitz heard Dennis's sharp intake of breath as the light faded. He was right: the nightlight in the apartment had been for Dennis, not his girlfriend. Still standing by the door, he turned back to Dennis. 'For a man like you, I'd have expected more sympathy for the victims, Dennis. Like Peter Yang – a millionaire – whose failing was to have everything you ever wanted. Or Dr Sunny, whose failing wasn't actually that he was going to terminate a pregnancy but that he had the power to change your future.'

Dennis watched Fitz take his hand away from the light switch to light a cigarette. Then he looked across the table at Janet and Wise. 'This', he said with something of his former arrogance, 'is all wind and piss. You've got the wrong man.'

Neither of them replied. Janet smiled her glacial smile. Wise looked bored. But behind their respective façades, they were both wondering what on earth was going on. With experience of Fitz's unorthodox methods, Wise was confident he knew what he was doing. Janet was concerned that those methods were bordering on intimidation.

202

Then Fitz reached for the switch again and turned it off. The only light in the room was the faint glow through the frosted glass of the door – enough to show the beads of perspiration on Dennis's forehead. And the only sound in the room was that of Dennis's suddenly laboured breathing.

'The Victorians', said Fitz in his best lecture-tour voice, 'came by boat, you know. Pissing themselves with glee. You know why they called this the Fragrant Harbour? It wasn't the herbs and spices, wasn't the shell-fish.' He leaned forward and rubbed his thumb against his forefinger. 'It was the sound of crisp pound notes and cash registers.'

Dennis was breathing more rapidly now, taking pained, shallow gulps of air. 'Turn it on,' he said in a quiet, childlike voice. Opposite him, Janet felt a first, faint twinge of pity for the man. Then she recalled her first opinion of Dennis and quelled it immediately. Embarrassed behind her mask of inscrutability, she continued to stare at the man opposite her.

'We came,' continued Fitz, 'we saw, we conquered. Like you, Dennis. Big boys' playground. You only had to *be* here to look successful to your family.'

Dennis looked up at Janet with pleading eyes. 'Can you get him to . . .'

'We should never have been here in the first place, you see. India was a doddle because the masses were passive. We pillaged the commonwealth without a squeak.' Fitz's words were casual, his voice conversational, but his eyes were intent; fixed on the increasingly desperate man before him. He knew that what he was doing, not what he was saying, was the issue: forcing Dennis to sit in the darkness, teasing his Achilles' heel.

'But', he continued, 'we completely overstretched ourselves coming this far out. Know why? They want to succeed more than we do.' Fitz leaned towards the desk and crushed his cigarette in the ashtray. 'It's written all over your face, Dennis. Mine.' He pointed to Wise. 'His. *Gweilos* – white ghosts. We're visitors, Dennis. You could never belong here.'

'Turn it on! Turn it on!' The scream was accompanied by the scrape of Dennis's chair against the floor as he leaped to his feet. Sweating heavily, barely able to draw breath, he held his hands up to his eyes, then to his ears, clawing pathetically for a return to his senses.

And then the light that Dennis craved appeared as the door opened and Gordon Ellison burst in. He snatched at the light switch and looked around, furious, at the blinking faces. At Fitz, annoyed at the intrusion; at Wise, impassive behind his glasses; and at Dennis, with his soaking shirt collar, his tears and his trembling hands.

'DCI Cheung,' he snapped. 'May we have a word?'

Janet nodded and rose to her feet. She was both annoyed and relieved by the interruption: annoyed because she had known they were getting close to the truth, relieved because she feared Dennis would crack completely before they arrived at it.

She nodded an apology to Fitz and followed Ellison into the corridor, closing the door behind her.

A few yards from the interrogation room, Ellison stopped and rounded on her. 'DCI Cheung, I want you to stop this bloody pantomime. Now!'

Janet took a deep breath. 'I think that would be a mistake, sir.'

'Frankly I don't give a shit, DCI Cheung. Get him out!'

'No.' This time there was no attempt at apology; no recognition of Ellison's rank, merely insubordination. And Janet didn't even wait for a response. She turned on her heel and went back to the interrogation room, leaving Ellison more stunned than angry. Then he, too, walked away – to phone the Commissioner.

To Janet's annoyance, she found that Fitz had continued to question Dennis during her brief absence. But at least he had kept the light on. The darkness, anyway, was no longer needed. He had established what he wanted.

'When I said "family",' he was saying as Janet sat down, 'you said "him". When I said "parents", you said "him".' Fitz jabbed at the photograph of the slim brunette in the print dress. 'You've got a mother: your father didn't carve you out of chipwood. But why doesn't she count as family, Dennis?'

Him, thought Janet. Why didn't I notice that peculiarity? She looked over at Wise. He nodded and gave a small smile. He had also missed the vital reference.

Fitz sat down again and dragged his chair even closer to Dennis.

'Who do you reckon you favour, Dennis? Father or mother?'

'Him.'

'But you change your hair colour. Before that you must've been the spitting image of her.'

'No.'

Fitz tapped at the photograph again. 'But you are.'

'No. You've got the wrong man.'

'Hmm. The man we're looking for killed his victims in the dark before he tied their hands. Like this, Dennis. Like *this*.' Dennis flinched at the sight of Fitz's clasped hands. 'Is that anyone you know, Dennis?'

'No. Please . . .'

'You're terrified of the dark and you're ashamed of your mum. Is that common in Romford?'

Dennis leaned forward and buried his head in his hands. 'Don't,' he moaned.

But Fitz did. He bent towards Dennis and pulled his arms away. The younger man's face was streaked with new tears. And now Fitz was so close that Dennis could feel his breath. 'What did you see in the dark, Dennis?'

Dennis snatched his hands back and, sitting bolt upright again, covered his eyes with them. 'Please don't do this.'

'What did you see?'

'I can't', replied Dennis in a suddenly childlike voice, 'see anything.'

'Dennis.' Fitz's voice was different too. Softer. 'You can't scare me. You're trembling. Come on. I can help you. Just tell me.'

206

'I can't see anything.'

'If I make a call, who do I speak to first – mother or father?'

To what, wondered Janet, was Fitz referring? The situation in Hong Kong – or the episode in the darkness that so haunted the young Dennis Philby?

It was the latter. 'It'll tear him apart,' whined Dennis the child. 'He'll blame me.'

'He doesn't know?'

'No.'

'Your secret? Yours and your mother's?'

The mother. What had the mother *done*? Unaware of the discomfort, Janet dug her nails into her palms again.

Fitz knew. The refusal to acknowledge her. The frightened boy in the dark. The shame. The photographs of the parents – and the hair dye Benny Ho had found tucked away in the bathroom of Dennis's apartment.

'He doesn't know that you're someone else's son?'

'I'm not!' The vehemence of Dennis's response shocked Janet and Wise more than Fitz's extraordinary question. He glared at Fitz, hatred radiating from his cold blue eyes.

'The older you get,' said Fitz, picking up the mother's photograph in one hand and the father's in the other, 'the less like him you look. You had *her* colouring – until you changed it. But your looks are embarrassing. Every time you shove your face in a mirror you're seeing the face of the man your mother's sleeping with. And one day your dad's going to look at you sideways and click. He's going to click that your mother and you have been lying to him all these years. And you're the one he'll blame, Dennis.'

Dennis was crying freely; piteous tears of confused, childish despair. 'It wasn't my fault,' he sobbed.

'I know. And you didn't tell him.'

Dennis stared, unseeing, across the room, and across the decades to the shame of his childhood. 'I didn't know what was going on. We were going', he added with bitter venom, '"to the library".'

'You were her alibi? Libraries aren't dark.'

Dennis snorted. 'Garages are.'

'What kind of garages?'

'Repair shop.'

Fitz paused for a second, willing Dennis to stay with the memory.

'You're smelling the petrol?' he prompted. 'Smelling the oil? You're pushed into a corner? Pushed in the office?'

Good God, thought Janet. What kind of mother did that to her son? Involved him in her duplicity, not caring what he saw or felt? Shutting him in the dark.

'"Play with your books, Dennis, read your books."' It was Fitz who said the words, but they were the right ones; the same ones that Dennis's mother had used. 'But how can you read when they put the lights out, Dennis?' Fitz leaned forward again, remembering the open-plan apartment, the light, the lack of doors. 'You can't do anything when they put the lights out because they've locked the door. You're shaking the handle, screaming to be let out. All you can hear is gasping, groaning. That's your mother out there, Dennis. What the hell's happening to her?'

Dennis's whole face was now a mask of hatred. But the emotion was no longer directed at Fitz; it had turned inwards, into the past to the dark place where his flighty, glamorous, uncaring mother had taken him and left him while she satisfied her lust.

'She's shagging him,' spat Dennis.

'You're only guessing. It was dark.'

'I took a torch. The third time, I took a torch.'

'You saw him?'

Dennis nodded.

'Did she take you back there?'

'On Mondays.' Shame was written all over Dennis's face. '"Library Day."'

'But you stopped kicking at the door after a while?'

No response from Dennis.

Fitz looked reproachful. 'That man is banging your mum and you're letting it happen?'

I tried to stop her, screamed a voice in Dennis's head. *I tried. But she laughed and said it would kill him. Our little secret.*

Fitz knew what the voice was saying.

'You let it happen because she's telling you you'll hurt your dad if you open your mouth. The family'll fall apart, and you never want to cause that. So you sit in the dark with your torch and your books and you pretend you don't know what's going on, pretend it never crossed your mind how far back it went.' Fitz paused and peered at Dennis. 'Before you?' Then, with no response forthcoming, he shrugged and continued in the soft, mesmeric voice that kept Dennis in the past. 'You're driving to school. You're driving to school and your dad thinks you're not talking to him cos he's done something wrong. And then he's laughing cos he's running out of lists of things he could've done wrong. Then he gives up – but you still can't speak.' Fitz kept his eyes riveted on Dennis's face as he spoke, saw the nodding, then the confused shaking of the head. Had it happened like that? He didn't know. But he knew it had happened. The guilt gnawing away inside, ruining Dennis's relationship with his father. Ruining Dennis's ability to relate.

And at some point his father had found out. 'Then,' continued Fitz, 'on a Sunday afternoon, you get back from your nan's and he's looking at you like he hates you. *Really* hates you. You can't see *her*, but you can hear her crying somewhere. She's crying somewhere.'

No! screamed the voice, *she wasn't even crying.*

'Your nan walks you to school now and nobody ever says another word about it. But it takes what feels like years for him to open his mouth again. And when he does, his voice sounds different.'

Yes. Full of hatred.

'And when he gives you your first wodge of money to start your own business, you know exactly why he's doing it.'

'Yes.' Tears streaming down his face, Dennis looked at Fitz with a sad half-smile. He felt that this man understood. That he cared.

He was wrong.

210

'Dennis,' shouted Fitz in a harsher voice, 'this is bloody biblical! If you hadn't murdered three people you'd have me sobbing in a bloody bucket. You really would.'

Fitz's words brought Dennis back to the present with a terrible jolt. The awful image of real life assailed him.

'All you're giving me there', continued Fitz, 'is the highly digestible notion that *people aren't nice to each other!* Is that your secret? Is that your excuse?' Contempt written all over his face, he leaned back, as if trying to distance himself from the younger man. 'Three dead, three more families liquidized?'

Dennis looked at Fitz. Another betrayal. Why, always, betrayal? And why didn't people understand?

'When I left home,' he said, 'she left home. He's sitting there on his own – ten years he's been sitting on his own – and he's done *nothing wrong*.' Then he remembered the great event, his wonderful plan, and his features softened. 'When Su-Lin got pregnant, I knew that was my ticket home. I get a baby – something that's mine. Something I cherish.'

Oh God, thought Janet, bile rising in her throat.

'I take it back to England,' continued Dennis, recounting his beautiful dream, 'and show it to him. Not her – him. I'm showing him a beautiful family and wanting him to know I'm not like *her*. I want him to feel we belong to him.'

'But she wanted to abort?' Janet's harsh voice echoed round the room like the crack of a whip.

Dennis glared at her, hating her for being there, for

211

being real. Then he cleared his throat and wiped away the remaining tears. When he spoke again, his voice carried not hatred but mild reproach, a quiet sadness. 'She didn't think we were ready. She'd no idea how ready I was. I'm saying this is my biggest chance and she's just not buying it.' He shook his head. 'The business is bombing, the colony's bombing, and I've spent just about as long away from home as I can.' Then the hardness came back. 'I knew she'd never be solid about it; I couldn't trust her word that she wouldn't go off and do it behind my back.' He stared at Janet, challenge implicit in the look. 'She was never a good liar.'

'Was?'

'Yes. She's dead. I killed her.'

It was Wise who broke the ensuing, shocked silence. 'What about the others?'

Dennis nodded. 'Peter Yang; Dr Sunny; the civil servant.'

'You'll repeat that', asked Janet, 'in front of a lawyer?'

'Yes.'

'Where's her body?'

Dennis turned to Fitz. The distant expression was back, and with it the far-away voice. 'I've lost a wife and child, like he lost a wife and child. So when he comes to see me, we'll understand each other.'

Chapter Nine

'He's lying.'

'*Lying?*' Janet nearly laughed. Fitz, presumably, was joking. An untimely, tactless joke to boot. Jokes were the last thing she needed. She felt exhausted, emotionally drained. Presumably Dennis Philby felt a great deal worse. The confessions Fitz had wrenched from him had been painful, drawn-out – and true.

But it was Ellison who replied. Still annoyed at Janet for her blatant insubordination, he was, as ever, prepared to forgive anything in the name of a good result. And Janet had just spent the last few minutes telling him about the spectacular result achieved in the interview room. Furthermore, Benny Ho and the forensics experts had achieved another one during their search of Dennis's car.

'He's not lying,' Ellison sneered. 'Forensics found human hair in the boot of his car. And blood. We know it's her type from the doctor's records.'

Fitz held up both hands in the air. 'Please. Just listen to me. This is Camberwick Green. What he confessed to is a fantasy.'

Ellison shot him a withering look. 'His fantasies are all tagged in the morgue if you need another look.'

'No! Her. *Her*. If she was dead, he'd have confessed in the first five seconds.'

Swigging from a can of Coke, Wise nodded his agreement. Janet's doubt gave way to curiosity. Ellison, however, was merely irritated.

'Dr Fitzgerald,' he sighed, 'we needed a confession. We got a confession. Why the hell would he . . .'

'Why do you think, you vacuous shite?'

The force and animosity of Fitz's words took everyone by surprise. Benny Ho looked extremely shocked. Wise was grinning. Janet was trying her hardest not to.

It was the first time anyone had levelled such an accusation at Ellison. People said much worse behind his back, but then Ellison was too arrogant to spare a thought about what others might be saying, feeling or doing. It had certainly never occurred to him that they might criticize him. He was so surprised by Fitz's insult that it took him a few seconds to reply. When he did find his voice, it was accompanied by intense, overt dislike.

'You've just pissed in your chips, Doctor. Please leave the building.' He pointed a headmasterly finger towards the door. 'Now.'

214

Fitz took no notice. 'She's alive and he knows where she is.' Behind him, Benny Ho whispered something to Janet. Then he handed her a jar of capsules. When Janet turned back to face Ellison, she found it hard to keep the grin off her face and the triumph from her voice. 'Folic acid,' she said, holding up the jar.

'What?' Annoyed that his rage against Fitz was being diluted, Ellison shot her an impatient, irritated glance.

'Iron pills for pregnant women.'

'So.'

'They were found on Philby when he was arrested. And *he's* not pregnant, is he?'

'Wherever he's got her,' said Fitz, pressing home the advantage, 'he was planning to keep her there till she gave birth.' There was no nuance of triumph in his voice, no trace of one-upmanship in the look he gave Ellison; just a deadly seriousness. 'And without him, she dies.'

Ellison looked away. He wanted not to believe Fitz; wanted to shout at him for wasting time, for twisting the truth. Yet he knew those feelings were fuelled by personal animosity. And he knew what Fitz was implying.

'I take it you mean that if we keep him in detention, she'll die?'

'Yes.'

Ellison felt a great weariness come over him. This was not supposed to be happening. It shouldn't be ending this way. And he didn't want to make the decision.

'I can't', he said, 'take responsibility for letting him go.'

No, thought Fitz. But then you can't take responsibility for anything, can you?

It was Janet who replied.

'If you wait for a Commissioner's decision, she's going to die.' She looked, coolly challenging, at the boss she despised. 'And if she dies, you take responsibility for both those lives.'

'But we have no guarantee', protested Ellison, 'that he'll lead us straight to her.'

'Leave it to me and I guarantee that he will.'

All heads turned to Fitz. 'And just how', drawled Ellison, 'are you going to do that?'

'By getting him a lawyer.'

'*What?*'

Fitz grinned. 'If we just let him go, if we give him a pat on the back and say "thanks, laddie, but you're right and we're wrong", he's going to smell a rat, isn't he?'

'Too bloody right,' said Wise. 'He confessed.'

'Exactly. So now we get him a lawyer who'll say – as any lawyer worth his salt *would* say – that we extracted the confession under duress. That we had no business conducting the interview in the first place.'

'You mean . . .?'

'Yeah.' Fitz looked around the room. They were in the 'bullpen' of police headquarters, the nerve centre of operations. Several policemen and women were typing on computers; others were discussing their current investigations: all were trying to pretend they weren't riveted by the heated discussion in the corner.

'Who wants to play the lawyer?' yelled Fitz.

216

'This really is most unethical . . .' began Ellison.

'And it's our only chance of finding the girlfriend,' snapped Janet. Then she noticed Sam Kai, one of her junior detectives, standing by the door. The expression on his face told her that he had followed every word of their conversation. But Janet was more interested in his hobbies than his expression. Sam was the current star of the Fin Lang Amateur Dramatics Society. Sam could act. Sam could play the lawyer.

He was also a quick learner. Already aware, as were most of his colleagues, of what a real lawyer would say both to and about a suspect who had been detained and questioned without legal representation, the words weren't difficult. Their delivery, however, had to be convincing.

The scenario concocted by Fitz would have amused Janet had the situation not been so grave. It involved her shouting at Fitz, berating him for his unorthodox and highly questionable methods of extracting a confession – and all within the hearing of Dennis Philby. A few days ago, she would have played the part without any prompting.

Half an hour after they had left Dennis to brood in silence under the watchful gaze of an armed policeman, they marched back down the corridor towards the interrogation room. Just as Ellison, standing in the corridor, had been able to hear the raised voices from within the room, so Dennis was aware of the argument erupting outside.

'He confessed,' protested Fitz.

'A confession extracted under duress. You're not qualified to take a confession. You're a civilian, Dr Fitzgerald, and you have just jeopardized the whole investigation!' Janet's heels, sharp staccato taps, echoed down the corridor, matching the anger in her voice.

And then Dennis heard the third voice. 'I want to see my client. I want to see him *now*.'

'That man is guilty.' Fitz was adamant.

'It doesn't matter whether he's guilty any more, you jerk,' snapped Janet. The footsteps had stopped. They were now standing outside Dennis's room. 'You put words into his mouth and you have screwed my case. I want you out of the building!'

Dennis sat bolt upright, his antennae straining to hear the reply.

It came from the lawyer. 'I want to see my client. Now!'

And then the door opened.

Dennis looked at the stranger who was first into the room. Smartly and expensively suited, he looked every inch the thrusting young lawyer. Although clearly angered by the ineptitude of the police, his expression changed to one of concerned sympathy as he walked towards Dennis and sat down opposite him. Dennis's own expression was blank.

'Mr Philby,' began the lawyer, 'my name's Sam Kai. I've been assigned to represent you.' He looked straight into Dennis's eyes. 'I'm going to get you out of here.'

Dennis's head was spinning. Frowning, he stared back at the lawyer. Then he looked towards Janet, standing

218

tight-lipped at the door, clearly having difficulty suppressing her rage and disappointment. Fitz hadn't come
into the room with her. Dennis was pleased about that.
He never wanted to see the odious man again. Then a
slow smile spread across his face as he realized that the
wish could become a reality. His confusion, his startled
disbelief, gave way to relief.

'You've been asked to make a statement on tape?'
asked the lawyer.

Dennis nodded.

Sam Kai shook his head. 'That's not going to happen.
You don't say anything to anyone until we've talked.
Alone.' The last word, although spoken to Dennis, was
obviously intended for Janet. So were the next ones.
'They've got no evidence against you. They had no right
to hold you in the first place. Why on earth', he asked
incredulously, 'didn't you call a lawyer?'

'I . . . I didn't. I tried, but . . .'

Disgusted, Sam Kai turned to Janet. 'Could my client
go now, please? *Now*.' It was the first, and probably the
last time he would ever be able to speak to his boss like
that. He relished the tiny moment.

Janet, amused behind her stern façade, nodded her
assent.

Kai extended an arm across the table, gesturing for
Dennis to stand up.

'They've got my car,' said Dennis in sudden panic.
'They took my car away.'

Kai steered him out into the corridor. 'You get your
things, Mr Philby. I'll handle the car.'

Dennis almost broke into a run, so anxious was he to be on his way.

Behind him, Janet stood watching, her features creased with worry. This was it. The cars were ready to tail Dennis. The helicopters had been alerted. But how could Fitz be so sure that Dennis would lead them to Su-Lin Tang? What made him think that he wouldn't just try to make a run for it, to get the hell away from the mess he had created for himself? Janet wasn't even sure that Philby was capable of rational thought any more. Confused after his interrogation, he might even have forgotten about Su-Lin. Or he might, after so many betrayals, not care about her any more.

Five minutes later Fitz demonstrated why he was so sure that Dennis would lead them to Su-Lin.

'Oh,' he said, affecting surprise that he should chance to be walking to the main entrance of the police station at the same time as Dennis was collecting his car keys from the Custody Desk in reception. 'So they're letting you go, Dennis?'

Dennis couldn't bear to look at Fitz. The sound of his voice alone made him shake with hatred.

Fitz reached the bottom of the staircase. Janet Lee Cheung was behind him.

'Me too,' he said to Dennis's back. 'No chance of a lift, I suppose?'

Dennis went rigid. 'I don't want to talk to this man,' he said through pursed lips. The Custody Officer, unaware of the play being enacted in front of him, looked over to Janet for guidance.

'Car keys!' screamed Dennis. 'Car keys!'

Janet nodded. Relieved to be seeing the back of the hysterical Dennis, the Custody Officer handed them over.

And then, as Dennis turned towards the door, Fitz struck again.

'You're a liar, Dennis,' he sneered. 'And I know your secret.'

Dennis whirled round. 'What?'

Fitz came closer. 'Su-Lin isn't dead. You haven't killed her. But do you know what the real tragedy is?'

'Shut up!'

'You're too late.' There was a triumph, a vicious glee in Fitz's voice as he leaned even closer to Dennis. 'She's already had the termination.'

'What?'

'Ten days ago, when you were in Macau. She was making all your decisions for you, Dennis. She didn't trust you.'

Dennis's mouth opened in a silent agony. His body twisted and lurched towards Fitz and his face, so distorted with shock, was barely recognizable as that of Dennis Philby. Then, with a supreme effort of will, he managed to control himself.

'You bloody liar!' was all he said. Then he turned and ran out of the police station.

Fitz and Janet watched him go. Watched his 'lawyer' try frantically to keep up with him as he belted across the forecourt to his car. Then Fitz turned round, his expression grim but certain.

'Now he'll go to her.'

Ellison, accompanied by Wise, was standing at the top of the stairs. Both had witnessed the scene below: Fitz's lies; Dennis's anguish. Ellison was horrified.

'Honestly . . . in my position, would you do this?'

Wise shrugged. 'Oh, I'm always taking risks, me. I'm known for it in Manchester. Ask any bugger.' As with Fitz, the lie tripped easily off his tongue.

They all went in the same car. Another, stationed outside the forecourt, had followed Dennis the minute he'd torn away into the traffic. Dozens more throughout the city had been alerted to the possibility that the BMW might once more be on the move. Police helicopters were already airborne. And this time, Kowloon was also ready. Janet was taking absolutely no chances. If they lost him, they would lose Su-Lin. Fitz's final statement to Dennis had convinced her of that.

It was easy to tail Dennis. He kept his hand almost permanently on the horn, screaming for other drivers to get out of the way. He even skipped two red lights in his haste to reach his destination. And, after twenty minutes, it looked like that destination was somewhere in Kowloon.

Janet was driving and talking into her radio at the same time. Fitz sat tight-lipped beside her. Ellison was too keyed-up even to notice that he had been demoted into the back seat with Wise.

'Don't follow him!' shouted Janet into the radio as

Dennis's route was confirmed. 'Don't go into the tunnel. We have two cars tailing from the other side. He's not stupid.' Then she turned to Fitz. 'We'll stay this side, too. Until we know exactly where he's headed.'

Fitz nodded. Yet Janet's words sparked a tiny flame of doubt in his mind. *He's not stupid.* But exactly how clever was he? Would he, alone in the car, calm down enough to contemplate the likelihood of his being followed? And if he did, what would he do about it?

Across the water, safely at the other end of the tunnel, Dennis was breathing more easily. The overriding desperation to get as far away from Fitz as possible had abated. His white-knuckle fever caused by the traffic was fading, calmed by the swift and unhindered drive through the tunnel. He was still consumed with fury at Su-Lin for her ultimate betrayal, still bent on reaching her as quickly as possible. Yet there was a rationality in his rage – and a growing suspicion that he was being tailed. That icy bitch of a detective, quietly watchful where her fat colleague had been aggressive, had been furious that her investigation had been ruined, livid at Dennis's release. But she hadn't looked the type to give in that easily. She would be watching still. Dennis knew it.

And then he saw the helicopter. It was flying high and way to the right of him – but it was just near enough for Dennis to read the insignia, the bold blue letters on the red body of the craft: POLICE.

With the desperate cunning of the hunted, Dennis

didn't waste a second. He pulled into a side-street on the left, a narrow thoroughfare that, like so many of the streets on Kowloon, was festooned with gaudy signs hanging from the buildings above. They would render the traffic almost invisible from overhead.

But not from in front or behind. Dennis screeched to a halt and leaped out of the car, not even bothering to close the door behind him. If he was being followed at a distance or if he was being hunted from the air, his pursuers would have details of the BMW; they would know the registration and the colour. He needed an anonymous vehicle. He needed to lose himself in the crowd – and there was a very easy way to do that.

He didn't have to wait more than a few seconds for a taxi. The red and white vehicle, an identical clone of thousands of other Hong Kong taxis, juddered to a halt beside him as he held out his hand. Dennis leaped into the back seat and slammed the door behind him. He waited until the unsuspecting driver half-turned to listen for directions before he lunged forward.

It was the driver's total surprise that stopped him yelling as he saw the hands descending. Then, after his head cracked against the hard plastic steering-wheel, he was unable to make any sound at all.

Dennis was in the front seat in seconds. He hauled the prone body out of the vehicle and dumped it without ceremony on the pavement. Then he took the driver's place, gunned the engine and sped down the street. The whole episode had happened so quickly that the ten witnesses were still in shock as the vehicle disappeared from view. Then they began to react, each in a different way. The majority disappeared as quickly as the taxi, melting into the throng. 'Getting involved' terrified them. They were scared of the police – even more so of the Triads. Anyway, they hadn't seen anything.

Two young men were kinder. They bent down to the unconscious taxi-driver. One of them felt for a pulse. The other mopped ineffectively at the gash on his forehead. And then the man who had seen the whole thing from the sanctuary of his first-floor apartment reached for his phone and called the police.

Janet didn't believe the first call. They had stopped, half a mile from the tunnel entrance, to await confirmation of Dennis's exit from the tunnel. That confirmation came from the helicopter, from the policeman with the high-powered binoculars who was monitoring the progress of the BMW.

Janet breathed a sigh of relief. Although she knew Dennis was unarmed, she had been worried when he had disappeared to make the short journey under the water. She wanted him in her sights for every second of his journey.

And then the call came; the unbelievable news.

'*What?*' she yelled into the radio. Her three passengers, already on tenterhooks, jumped in their seats and turned to her. Her face was deathly white. 'You *can't* have!' she screamed. But they had. The crackling voice on the radio repeated its shameful message.

Janet turned to Fitz. 'They've lost him.'

It was Ellison who replied. 'I knew it!' he shouted. 'We should never have let him go. Jesus Christ! Of all the incompetent, blundering inefficiency . . . I mean, what the bloody hell do we do now?'

Janet stared fixedly ahead. She couldn't bear to look at any of her passengers, couldn't bear to talk to Ellison. Anyway, there was nothing to say. She started the engine and pulled out into the traffic, towards Kowloon. Discretion was no longer needed. The surveillance had failed. The police on the other side of the water needed all the help they could get in the desperate search for their fugitive.

The next call came barely a minute later. Janet snatched at the radio, gripped it, her knuckles white. Beside her, Fitz watched intently. She talked in Cantonese, but her body language was universal. He saw the tension leave her shoulder, the slow smile of relief begin to play at the corners of her mouth. Then the disappointment returned. The smile died and was replaced by tight-lipped anger.

Distraught, she turned her haunted eyes to Fitz. 'He's changed vehicles,' she snapped. 'He's taken a taxi – and we don't know the licence plate.'

Ellison, predictably, greeted the news with expletives; Fitz and Wise with silent panic. They knew what that meant. They knew they were now looking for the proverbial needle in a haystack. And if they needed any confirmation, they could find it outside their car. Alongside them, a string of identical taxis swarmed past, teeming worker ants unaware of the drama in their colony.

*

Janet drove to where Dennis had abandoned his car. It seemed as good a place as any; it gave the impression of positive action. Yet they all knew it was illusory and that the chances of finding Dennis again were practically nil.

Fitz remained in the car while the others joined the officers already beside Dennis's own, abandoned vehicle. Ellison stomped around outside the car, muttering angrily and throwing accusatory looks at Fitz. Janet tried to instil calm over the panic. Wise just stood, jangling the coins in his pocket, looking bemused. Fitz appeared to be doing absolutely nothing, a fact which enraged Ellison even further. To illustrate the point, he came back to the car and kicked the rear wheel in frustration. Fitz didn't notice. He continued with what he was doing: thinking.

Then Janet returned to the driver's seat and re-established radio contact with the other vehicles; with the cars and the helicopters. The look she gave Fitz a moment later told him all he wanted to know. There was nothing: no sighting of Dennis Philby.

Ellison's flushed face appeared at Fitz's window.

'So? What does the psychologist recommend? If you're so bloody good at tapping into Dennis Philby's mind, can't you tell us what he's up to?'

Fitz looked, without animosity, at the other man. Ellison was now so reduced in his estimation that he no longer merited a loss of temper. He didn't merit a lingering look either. Fitz turned to Janet, bestowing on her the fruits of his recent thoughts.

227

'What we've got to think is, what's in Kowloon for him? If we're talking about that much pride, there's only one person left to show it to – his father. He wants to take Su-Lin to England.'

'Tough shit!' snorted Ellison from outside. 'We've got all his documents. He'll never get out of the country – let alone into another.'

'But what if he doesn't have to show his face? He moves parcels, shifts boxes all the time for a living. Janet,' he added, 'd'you have a map in the car?'

Janet nodded in the direction of the glove compartment. Fitz opened it and extracted a large map of the whole territory. Realizing it was too unwieldy to be unfolded in the car, Fitz joined Ellison outside and spread the map on the bonnet. Janet accompanied him, a pensive frown creasing her features.

'There was', she recalled, 'an Export Order booked from his factory. The documents were on the wall.' Why, she wondered, hadn't she thought of that, realized that it might have some significance? She had been too preoccupied with notions of Dennis concealing Su-Lin – not transporting her, as Fitz was suggesting, to another country.

'But the guy's gone bankrupt. What the hell's he supposed to be shipping?'

Janet, Fitz and now Wise looked at Ellison – all of them with pitying expressions.

Belatedly, the penny dropped. 'Oh. I see. You mean . . . you mean he's trying to *ship* her to England?'

Janet hadn't wanted to articulate the macabre

thought. It was too hideous to contemplate: Su-Lin trapped like a caged animal. Penned in for weeks. Pregnant. Hiding someone in a secluded waterway, in a quiet inlet was one thing: sending them on a six-week voyage was quite another. It was a slow, lingering and inhuman death sentence.

'He'd have to join her,' pointed out Wise.

'Dennis Philby?' intoned Fitz. 'The man who's afraid of the dark. He wouldn't last a minute.'

'No,' said Janet, 'that's just what I was thinking. But then', she added with a sidelong glance at Fitz, 'his plans have changed, haven't they?'

'Mmm.'

'What do you mean?' Again Ellison was behind the others.

'He's no longer interested in protecting Su-Lin, in getting her out of the country,' said Wise, thinking aloud. 'He thinks she's betrayed him like all the others. He doesn't think he's got a baby any more.'

'Oh, I *see*.' Ellison turned his mocking face to Fitz. 'Thanks to Dr Fitzgerald, he's now going to kill her instead, is he? And', he added with an expansive yet hopeless gesture, 'we haven't a clue where he is! Great. That's just great! I told you', he said, suddenly vicious, 'that you should never have invented the abortion.'

Fitz shrugged. 'It was the only way to make absolutely sure he'd go to her.' Then he turned away from Ellison and looked at the map.

'Where', he asked Janet, 'do they store freight in Hong

Kong?'

Janet rolled her eyes. 'How does "everywhere" sound?'

'But where would *Philby* store freight?' Fitz made no attempt to disguise his irritation.

'Again, everywhere.' Janet moved beside Fitz and pointed at the map. 'Philby Medical shipped stuff everywhere. If it was going to Australia, it would go from there,' she said, pointing at the map. 'Freight for mainland China would go from there and . . . oh!'

'Yes,' drawled Fitz. 'Freight to England?'

Suddenly animated, Janet studied the map with greater intensity.

'Several places, I think.'

'Let's say the Shipping Order you saw in his office is going to go through after all. Where was it booked from?'

Janet frowned, trying to remember. It had seemed so irrelevant at the time: a document detailing an anonymous cargo, destined never to reach any port. And how urgent it seemed now.

Janet was aware of the three men standing beside her, dwarfing her, intimidating her with their silence and the weight of their expectation.

'Tsing Yi,' she said suddenly. 'I'm sure that was it.' As she said the words, she indicated an area on the map on the western side of the Kowloon peninsula. The area, depressingly large, bore the legend 'Cargo Holding-Basin'.

'That's it,' said Fitz with more confidence than he felt. 'His second home. That's where he'll be.'

*

And that's where he was. The red and white taxi, protected and anonymous by the ubiquity of its breed, had sped unchallenged into the cargo holding-basin and straight to the aisle where Su-Lin's crate was stored. Dennis stopped some yards away and sat, staring with empty eyes at the red container. So; it had all been in vain. Su-Lin was no different from all the others. She had tried to trick him; had made him look a fool. And she had robbed him of his last chance to make his life worthwhile. His baby was dead. Now it was time for the mother to die.

It didn't take Dennis long to find the drums of kerosene. How careless people were, he thought as he rolled them towards Su-Lin's crate. Typical, though, of Hong Kong. Nobody thought of the possible consequences of leaving inflammable materials lying around. Nobody valued human life.

With a grim smile of satisfaction, Dennis rolled the first drum against the container and, muscles straining, pulled out the bung. The clear, acrid-smelling liquid poured out, gushing onto the uneven ground and finding its own course down which to flow. Most of it found the little gradient that led under Su-Lin's crate.

At first, Su-Lin couldn't identify the smell. She couldn't even decide if there *was* a smell – or if she was being visited by some new, tormented hallucination. Or if she had died and gone to hell.

And then she recognised that the overpowering smell assailing her nostrils was that of petrol and that hell – the real, blazing inferno of legend – was yet to come.

Barely able to move now, so dehydrated that she was no longer sweating, she managed to haul herself to her feet, to stumble to the outside wall of the container and to scream for help.

But it was all in vain. Dennis had gone to fetch another drum of kerosene. He wouldn't, anyway, have responded. For one thing, Su-Lin's desperate cries for help were no more than agonized gasps for air, and for another, he no longer cared. He no longer cared about anything. It was all over and soon they would both be dead.

At first he didn't even notice the helicopter. When it appeared, he was lining up the fifth drum of kerosene against the crate, looking over his shoulder as he did so. Then, nodding with satisfaction, he left the drum and walked back to the taxi. He hadn't emptied the drum: this was the one which, as he drove straight into it, would ignite the ball of fire that would kill them both.

As he opened the door of the taxi, he became aware of the helicopter. It was so close he wondered why he hadn't seen it before. Shading his eyes against the blazing sun, he looked up. He saw that it was the police helicopter and nodded. So they had found him – but too late. He jumped into the driving seat and slammed the door.

Above him, the police marksman had his sights on the car and his finger on the trigger. But in his ears he had the urgent voice of DCI Cheung over the radio.

'No guns!' she screamed. 'Put your guns away! We're in the cargo basin now. We have him in our sights!' The marksman relaxed his grip on the trigger – but the rifle remained trained on Dennis.

And then Janet's car, siren blaring, roared into the basin and screeched to a halt behind the little taxi. Ellison leaped out from the back seat and turned, signalling for the cars in their wake to stop behind them, to switch off their engines – and to put their guns away.

Fitz knew he only had one chance. He got out of the car and walked slowly towards the taxi, holding his hands in front of him. The gesture was partly pleading – but mainly to show he was unarmed. Dennis, he knew, was watching him in the rear-view mirror.

'Dennis!' he shouted when he was still twenty yards away. 'I lied. There was no abortion.' He was close enough to see that Dennis didn't react; that he seemed not even to have heard; that he was staring straight ahead at the red crate and the drums in front of it.

Fitz slowed his pace, moving to the right so that Dennis could see him out of the corner of his eye. 'Dennis . . .?'

Dennis turned and looked at him through eyes filled with blind hatred. Then he smiled and switched on the ignition.

Fitz's legs nearly gave way beneath him. As if aware of his sudden fear, Dennis smiled and revved the engine. The smell of the exhaust fumes mingled with the odour of the kerosene, so pungent it was almost visible, wafting towards them in the afternoon heat.

Then Dennis took his foot off the accelerator and pushed the car into gear. Taking advantage of the momentary silence, Fitz came closer.

'I *lied* to get you here, Dennis.' He no longer had to shout.

Dennis wavered. Fitz pounced on the hesitation.

'To help find Su-Lin,' he continued. 'Look,' he urged. 'Look at me, Dennis. We all lied. Your lawyer – he's a copper. We all lied because nobody wants her to die, Dennis.'

Dennis nodded. He didn't want to, didn't intend to listen to this man. Yet there was something in his voice that had to be heard.

Fitz took a deep breath. 'On the life of my children . . . my *children*, Dennis. She is still carrying your baby. If you needed any proof that you're worthy of a future, you've only to look at the woman.'

Dennis looked. But all he could see was the crate and the kerosene. Then, suddenly puzzled, he turned back to Fitz.

'Five years you've spent together, Dennis. Does she think you're a foreign body? No! She loves you. She's the only person you've ever known who didn't give a shit about your baggage.' *Make him feel wanted*, Fitz shouted to his inner self. *One of us.* 'If you're feeling pushed out again, that's none of her fault, Dennis.' He shook his head, smiling sadly, inviting Dennis to share his feelings. 'We should never have been here in the first place. It's not just *you*, Dennis.'

Dennis didn't say a word. He gazed at Fitz, totally expressionless, for what seemed like an eternity. Fitz held his breath – and his own, intense stare into Dennis's eyes.

The silence was almost tangible; the deafening noise of normality had ceased. It seemed like all Hong Kong was quiet, waiting respectfully for the future.

The sudden screech of the taxi's engine broke the calm. Dennis, too, was screaming as he drove towards the crate: shouting at his mother, his father, at Su-Lin and at the world. A world on which he had wanted so desperately to leave his mark, a permanent reminder of himself.

On the life of my children, she is still carrying your baby. Dennis didn't know where the words came from, or whose they were. All he knew was that they were ringing urgently in his ears as he thundered towards the crate.

Behind him, the horrified spectators saw the sudden, last-minute lurch to the right as Dennis wrenched at the wheel. For a moment, it looked as if the car would overturn as it teetered on two wheels. Then it righted itself and sped towards another, more distant crate.

It didn't need kerosene to turn the car into a ball of flames.

Su-Lin heard the explosion, just as she had heard the sound of the car racing towards her. She heard the roar of the flames – and she smelled the deadly, acrid fumes. Paralysed with fear, she sat slumped against the wall of her prison, awaiting the inferno that would engulf her.

It never came. Instead she heard voices; urgent voices shouting her name. Too weak and too bemused to reply, she remained motionless, wondering if she

235

were dreaming. Only when the voices were replaced by the sound of crowbars against the walls of the crate did she realize her nightmare had ended. And, as one side of the crate opened, blinding her with harsh sunlight, a sudden movement surprised her. It was a movement that heralded a new beginning – and it came from inside her body. Dennis Philby's baby, his last legacy and his one worthwhile gift to the world, was kicking gently inside her womb.

When they reached Su-Lin, she had slipped into unconsciousness. She was also filthy, her face was streaked with dirt and her lank hair was hanging in greasy tendrils around her shoulders. But her smile was beatific and one tender hand was resting on her belly.

She never met the man who saved her life; he might as well have been a real white ghost. In reality, he was a very angry one. Ellison sacked Fitz that very evening.